William Walton

A Narrative of the Captivity and Sufferings of Benjamin Gilbert and his Family

William Walton

A Narrative of the Captivity and Sufferings of Benjamin Gilbert and his Family

ISBN/EAN: 9783744657259

Printed in Europe, USA, Canada, Australia, Japan

Cover: Foto ©Andreas Hilbeck / pixelio.de

More available books at **www.hansebooks.com**

A

NARRATIVE

OF THE

CAPTIVITY

AND

SUFFERINGS

OF

BENJAMIN GILBERT

AND HIS

FAMILY;

WHO WERE SURPRISED BY THE INDIANS, AND
TAKEN FROM THEIR FARMS, ON THE FRON-
TIERS OF PENNSYLVANIA.

IN THE SPRING, 1780.

PHILADELPHIA, PRINTED:

LONDON:
Reprinted and Sold by JAMES PHILLIPS, George-
Yard, Lombard-ftreet.

M. DCC. XC.

P R E F A C E.

AS the captivity of Benjamin Gilbert's Family has been a fubject of much inquiry, and many of their friends were anxious to have a particular account of their fufferings; the following narrative is prefented to them and the publick, reciting the tranfactions as circumftantially as could be furnifhed from memory, after comparing accounts with each other on their return from Canada.

That their lives were preferved through the many threatening fcenes they paffed, whilft in the hands of the Indians, is to be afcribed, with gratitude and thankfulnefs, to the great Ruler of the univerfe, who can fay unto the fea, " Thus far fhalt thou go, and no fur- " ther." And though Benjamin Gilbert the elder, was permitted to fink under the weight of his fatigue and afflictions, he lived to be reftored to liberty, and breathed his laft in the arms of his affectionate wife.

To be caft into the power of favages, who, from infancy, are taught hardnefs of heart,

A 2   which

which deprives them of the common feelings of humanity, is enough to intimidate the firmeft mind : but when we hear of helplefs women and children torn from their homes, and dragged into the wildernefs, we fhudder at the thought, and are bound to acknowledge our infinite obligations to the Almighty, that we are fo much more enlightened than thofe unhappy wretches of the defert ; to moft of whom the glad tidings of the gofpel remains yet to be proclaimed : " Glory " to God in the higheft ; on earth peace, and " good will to men."

A N A R.

A

NARRATIVE

OF THE

CAPTIVITY

AND

SUFFERINGS

OF

BENJAMIN GILBERT

AND HIS

FAMILY.

BENJAMIN GILBERT, fon of Jofeph Gilbert, was born at Byberry, about 15 miles from the city of Philadelphia, in the year 1711, and received his education among the people called Quakers.

He refided at or near the place of his nativity for feveral years; during which time of refidence he married, and after the deceafe of his firft wife, he accomplifhed a fecond marriage with Elizabeth Peart, widow of Bryan Peart, and continued in this neighbourhood until the year 1775, when he removed with his family to a farm, fituate on Mahoning Creek, in Penn Townfhip, North-

A 3

ampton county, being the frontiers of Pennfylvania, not far from where Fort Allen was
erected. The improvements he carried on
here were according to the ufual manner of
new fettlements, convenience being princi-
pally attended to, his houfe and barn being
of logs; to this he had added a faw-mill, and
a commodious ftone grift-mill, which, as it
commanded the country for a confiderable
diftance, conduced in fome meafure to render
his fituation comfortable.

This fhort account may not be improper,
in order to intereft our feelings in the relation of the many fcenes of affliction the family were reduced to, when fnatched from
the pleafing enjoyment of the neceffaries and
conveniencies of life. The moft flattering
of our profpects are often marked with difappointment, expreffively inftructing us, that
we are all ftrangers and fojourners here, as
were our forefathers.

This family was alarmed on the 25th day
of the 4th Month, 1780, about fun-rife, by
a party of eleven Indians, whofe appearance
ftruck them with terror; to attempt an efcape was death, and a portion of diftrefs,
not eafy to be fupported, the certain attendant on the moft patient and fubmiffive conduct. The Indians, who made this incurfion,
were of different tribes or nations, who had
abandoned their country on the approach of
General Sullivan's army, and fled within
command

command of the Britifh forts in Canada,
promifcuoufly fettling within their neighbourhood; and, according to Indian cuftom
of carrying on war, frequently invading the
frontier fettlements, taking captive the weak
and defencelefs.

The names of thefe Indians, with their re-
fpective tribes, are as follow :

1. Rowland Monteur, 1ft captain.

2. John Monteur, fecond in command,
who was alfo ftiled captain : thefe two were
Mohawks, defcended of a French woman.

3. Samuel Harris, a Cayuga Indian.

4. John Hufton, and his fon } Cayugas
5. John Hufton, jun.

6. John Fox, of the Delaware nation. The
other 5 were Senecas.

At this place they made captives of the
following perfons :

1. Benjamin Gilbert, aged about 69 years
2. Elizabeth, his wife,   55
3. Jofeph Gilbert, his fon   41
4. Jeffe Gilbert, another fon,   19
5. Sarah Gilbert, wife to Jeffe,   19
6. Rebecca Gilbert, a daughter,   16
7. Abner Gilbert, a fon,   14
8. Elizabeth Gilbert, a daughter,   12

9. Thomas Peart, fon to Benjamin } 23
Gilbert's wife,

10. Benjamin Gilbert, a' fon of } 11
John Gilbert, of Philadelphia,

A 4   11. Andrew

11. Andrew Harrigar, of German defcent, hired by Benjamin Gilbert, } 26 years

12. Abigal Dodfon, (daughter of Samuel Dodfon, who lived on a farm near one mile diftance from the mill) who came that morning with grift, } 14

They then proceeded to Benjamin Peart's dwelling, about half a mile farther, and brought himfelf and family, viz.

13. Benjamin Peart, fon to Benjamin Gilbert's wife, } 27

14. Elizabeth Peart, his wife, 20

15. Their child about nine months old.

The prifoners were bound with cords, which the Indians brought with them, and in this melancholy condition left under a guard for the fpace of half an hour; during which time, the reft of the captors employed themfelves in plundering the houfe, and packing up fuch goods as they chofe to carry off, until they had got together a fufficient loading for three horfes, which they took, befides compelling the diftreffed prifoners to carry part of their plunder. When they had finifhed plundering, they began their retreat, two of their number being detached to fire the buildings, which they did without any exception of thofe belonging to the unhappy fufferers; thereby aggravating their diftreffes, as they could obferve the

flames,

flames, and the falling in of the roofs, from an adjoining eminence called Summer Hill. They caft a mournful look towards their dwellings, but were not permitted to ftop, until they had reached the further fide of the hill, where the party fat down to make a fhort repaft; but grief prevented the prifoners from fharing with them.

The Indians fpeedily put forwards from this place; as they apprehended they were not fo far removed from the fettlements, as to be fecure from purfuit. Not much further was a large hill, called Mochunk, which they fixed upon for a place of rendezvous: here they halted near an hour, and prepared fhoes or fandals, which they call mockafons, for fome of the children: confidering themfelves in fome degree relieved from danger, their fears abated, fo that they could enjoy their meal at leifure, which they ate very heartily. At their removal from this hill, they told the prifoners that Colonel Butler was no great diftance from them, in the woods, and that they were going to him.

Near the foot of the hill flows a ftream of water, called Mochunk Creek, which was croffed, and the fecond mountain paffed; the fteep and difficult afcent of which appeared very great to the much enfeebled and affrighted captives: they were permitted to reft themfelves for fome minutes, and then preffed on-

A 5   wards

wards to the broad mountain, at the foot of which runs Nefcaconnah Creek.

Doubly diſtreſſed by a recollection of paſt happineſs, and a dread of the miſeries they had now to undergo, they began the aſcent of this mountain with great anguiſh both of body and mind. Benjamin Gilbert's wife, diſpirited with the increaſing difficulties, did not expect ſhe was able to paſs this mountain on foot; but being threatened with death by the Indians if ſhe did not perform it, with many a heavy ſtep ſhe at length ſucceeded. The broad mountain is ſaid to be ſeven miles over in this place, and about ten miles diſtant from Benjamin Gilbert's ſettlement. Here they halted an hour, and then ſtruck into the Neſkapeck Path; the unevenneſs and ruggedneſs of which rendered it exceedingly toilſome, and obliged them to move forwards ſlowly. Quackac Creek runs acroſs the Neſkapeck Path, which leads over Piſmire Hill. At this laſt place they ſtopped to refreſh themſelves, and then purſued their march along the ſame path, through Moravian Pine Swamp, to Mahoniah Mountain, where they lodged, being the firſt night of their captivity.

It may furniſh information to ſome, to mention the method the Indians generally uſe to ſecure their priſoners; they cut down a ſapling as large as a man's thigh, and there-

in

in cut notches, in which they fix their legs, and over this they place a pole, croffing the pole on each fide with ftakes drove in the ground, and in the crotches of the ftakes they place other poles or riders, effectually confining the prifoners on their backs; befides which, they put a ftrap round their necks, which they faften to a tree: in this manner the night paffed. Their beds were hemlock branches ftrewed on the ground, and blankets for a covering, which was an indulgence fcarcely to have been expected from favages: it may reafonably be expected, that in this melancholy fituation, fleep was a ftranger to their eye-lids.

Benjamin Peart having fainted in the evening, occafioned by the fufferings he endured, was threatened to be tomahawked by Rowland Monteur.

26th. Early this morning they continued their route near the waters of Teropin Ponds. The Indians thought it moft eligible to feparate the prifoners in companies of two by two, each company under the command of a particular Indian, fpreading them to a confiderable diftance, in order to render a purfuit as impracticable as poffible. The old people, overcome with fatigue, could not make fo much expedition as their fevere tafk-mafters thought proper, but failed in their journey, and were therefore threatened with death by

the

the Indian under whofe direction they were placed: thus circumftanced, they refigned themfelves to their unhappy lot with as much fortitude as poffible. Towards evening the parties again met and encamped, having killed a deer, they kindled a fire, each one roafting pieces of the flefh upon fharpened fwitches. The confinement of the captives was the fame with the firft night; but, as they were by this time more refigned to the event, they were not altogether deprived of fleep.

27th. After breakfaft a council was held concerning the divifion of the prifoners, which being fettled, they delivered each other thofe prifoners who fell within their feveral allotments, given them directions to attend to the particular Indians whofe property they became. In this day's journey they paffed near Fort Wyoming, on the eaftern branch of Sufquehanna, about forty miles from their late habitation. The Indians, naturally timid, were alarmed as they approached this garrifon, and obferved great caution, not fuffering any noife, but ftepped on the ftones that lay in the path, left any footfteps fhould lead to a difcovery. Not far from thence is a confiderable ftream of water, emptying itfelf into Sufquehanna, which they croffed with great difficulty, it being deep and rapid, and continued here this night. Benjamin Gilbert, being bound faft with cords, underwent great fufferings.

28th.

28th. This morning the prifoners were all painted according to the cuftom among the Indians, fome of them with red and black, fome all red, and fome with black only : thofe whom they fmut with black, without any other colour, are not confidered of any value, and are by this mark generally devoted to death: although this cruel purpofe may not be executed immediately, they are feldom preferved to reach the Indian hamlets alive. In the evening they came to Sufquehanna, having had a painful and wearifome journey through a very ftony and hilly path. Here the Indians fought diligently for a private lodging-place, that they might be as fecure as poffible from any fcouting-parties of the white people. It is unneceffary to make further mention of their manner of lodging, as it ftill remained the fame.

29th. They went in fearch of the horfes which had ftrayed from them in the night, and after fome time found them. They then kept the courfe of the river, walking along its fide with difficulty. In the afternoon they came to a place where the Indians had directed four negroes to wait their return, having left them fome corn for a fubfiftence: thefe negroes had efcaped from confinement, and were on their way to Niagara, when firft difcovered by the Indians; being challenged by them, anfwered, " They were for the king," upon which they immediately received them into protection.

30th

30th. The negroes, who were added to the company the day before, began cruelly to domineer and tyrannife over the prifoners, frequently whipping them for their fport, and treating them with more feverity than even the Indians themfelves; having had their hearts hardened by the meannefs of their condition, and long fubjeċtion to flavery. In this day's journey they paffed the remains of the Indian town, Wyaloofing. The lands round thefe ruins have a remarkable appearance of fertility. In the evening they made a lodgment by the fide of a large creek.

5th Month 1ft. After croffing a confiderable hill, in the morning, they came to a place where two Indians lay dead. A party of Indians had taken fome white people, whom they were carrying off prifoners, they rofe upon the Indians in the night, killed four of them, and then effeċted their efcape. The women were fent forwards, and the men prifoners commanded to draw near and view the two dead bodies, which remained (the other two being removed); they ftaid to obferve them a confiderable time, and were then ordered to a place where a tree was blown down. Death appeared to be their doom; but after remaining in a ftate of fad fufpenfe for fome time, they were ordered to dig a grave; to effeċt which, they cut a fapling with their tomahawks, and fharpened one end, with which

which wooden inftrument one of them broke the ground, and the others caft the earth out with their hands, the negroes being permitted to beat them feverely whilft they were thus employed. After interring the bodies, they went forwards to the reft, and overtook them as they were preparing for their lodging. They were not yet releafed from their fapling confinement.

2d. Having fome of their provifions with them, they made an early meal, and travelled the whole day. They croffed the eaft branch of Sufquehanna towards evening, in canoes, at the place where General Sullivan's army had paffed it in their expedition. Their en-campment was on the weftern fide of this branch of the river; but two Indians, who did not crofs it, fent for Benjamin Gilbert, jun. and Jeffe Gilbert's wife; and as no probable caufe could be affigned why it was fo, the defign was confidered as a very dark one, and was a grievous affliction to the others.

3d. The morning however difpelled their fears, when they had the fatisfaction of fee-ing them again, and underftood they had not received any treatment harder than their ufual fare. The horfes fwam the Sufque-hanna, by the fide of the canoe. This day the Indians in their march found a fcalp, and took it along with them, as alfo fome old corn, of which they made a fupper. They

frequently

frequently killed deer, and by that means supplied the company with meat, being almost the only provisions they ate, as the flour they took with them was expended.

4th. The path they travelled this morning was but little trodden, which made it difficult for those, who were not acquainted with the woods, to keep in it. They crossed a creek, made up a large fire to warm themselves by, and then separated into two companies, the one taking the Westward Path, with whom were Thomas Peart, Joseph Gilbert, Benjamin Gilbert, jun. and Jesse Gilbert's wife Sarah; the others went more to the north, over rich level land. When evening came, inquiry was made concerning the four captives who were taken in the Westward Path, and they were told, that " These " were killed and scalped, and you may ex- " pect the same fate to night." * Andrew Harrigar was so terrified at the threat, that he resolved upon leaving them, and as soon as it was dark, took a kettle with pretence of bringing some water, and made his escape under favour of the night: he was sought after by the Indians as soon as they observed him to be missing.

* Andrew Harrigar endured many hardships in the woods, and at length returned to the settlements, and gave the first authentic intelligence of Benjamin Gilbert and his family to their friends.

5th.

5th. In the morning the Indians returned ; their fearch for Andrew Harrigar being happily for him unfuccefsful : the prifoners who remained, were therefore treated with great feverity on account of his efcape, and were often accufed of being privy to his defign. Captain Rowland Monteur carried his refentment fo far, that he threw Jeffe Gilbert down, and lifted his tomahawk to ftrike him, which the mother prevented, by putting her head on his forehead, befeeching him to fpare her fon : this fo enraged him, that he turned round, kicked her over, and tied them both by their necks to a tree, where they remained until his fury was a little abated ; he then loofed them, and not long after bid them pack up and go forwards. They paffed through a large pine fwamp, and about noon reached one of the Kittareen towns, which was defolated. Not far from this town, on the fummit of a mountain, there iffues a large fpring, forming a very confiderable fall, and runs very rapidly in an irregular winding ftream down the mountain's fides. They left this place, and took up their lodging in a deferted wigwam covered with bark, which had formerly been part of the Shipquagas.

6th, 7th, 8th. They continued thefe three days in the neighbourhood of thefe villages, which had been deferted upon General Sullivan's approach. Here they lived well, having,

ing, in addition to their ufual bill of fare, plenty of turnips and potatoes, which had remained in the ground, unnoticed by the army. This place was the hunting ground of the Shipquagas; and whenever their induftry prompted them to go out a hunting, they had no difficulty to procure as many deer as they defired.

Roaft and boiled meat, with vegetables, afforded them plentiful meals; they alfo caught a wild turkey, and fome fifh, called fuckers. Their manner of catching fifh, was, to fharpen a ftick, and watch along the rivers until a fifh came near them, when they fuddenly pierced him with the ftick, and brought him out of the water.

Here were a number of colts, fome of them were taken, and the prifoners ordered to manage them, which was not eafily done.

9th. When they renewed their march, they placed the mother upon a horfe that feemed dangerous to ride, but fhe was preferved from any injury. In this day's journey they came to Meadow Ground, where they ftaid the night, the men being confined as before related, and the negroes lay near them for a guard.

10th. A wet fwamp, that was very troublefome, lay in their road; after which they had to pafs a rugged mountain, where there was no path. The underbrufh made it hard labour for

for the women to travel ; but no excuſe would avail with their ſevere maſters, and they were compelled to keep up with the Indians, however great the fatigue : when they had paſſed it, they tarried a while for the negroes who had lagged behind, having ſufficient employ to attend to the colts that carried the plunder. When all the company met together, they agreed to rendezvous in an adjoining ſwamp.

11th. A long reach of ſavannas and low ground rendered this day's route very fatiguing and painful, eſpecially to the women : Elizabeth Peart's huſband not being allowed to relieve her by carrying the child, her ſpirits and ſtrength were ſo exhauſted that ſhe was ready to faint ; the Indian, under whoſe care ſhe was, obſerving her diſtreſs, gave her a violent blow. When we compare the temper and cuſtoms of theſe people, with thoſe of our own colour, how much cauſe have we to be thankful for the ſuperiority we derive from the bleſſings of civilization.

It might truly be ſaid, days of bitter ſorrow, and weariſome nights, were appointed the unhappy captives.

12th. Their proviſions began to grow ſcant, having paſſed the hunting grounds : the want of proper food to ſupport them, which might render them more capable of enduring their daily fatigue, was a heavy trial, and

was

was much increafed by their confinement at night. Elizabeth Gilbert was reduced fo low, that fhe travelled in great pain all this day, riding on horfeback in the morning, but towards evening fhe was ordered to alight, and walk up a hill they had to af-cend; the pain fhe fuffered, together with want of food, fo overcame her, that fhe was feized with a chill : the Indians adminiftered fome flour and water boiled, which afforded her fome relief.

13th. Laft night's medicine being repeat-ed, they continued their march, and after a long walk, were fo effectually worn down, that they halted. The pilot, John Hufton, the elder, took Abner Gilbert with him, (as they could make more expedition than the reft) to procure a fupply of provifions to relieve their neceffity.

14th. The mother had fuffered fo much, that two of her children were obliged to lead her. Before noon they came to Canadofago, where they met with Benjamin Gilbert, jun. and Jeffe Gilbert's wife Sarah, two of the four who had been feparted from them ten days paft, and taken along the Weftern Path : this meeting afforded them great fatisfaction ; the doubt and uncertainty of their lives be-ing fpared often diftreffing their affectionate relations.

John Hufton, jun. the Indian, under whofe care Benjamin Gilbert was placed, defigning
to

to difpatch him, painted him black ; this exceedingly terrified the family, but no intreaties of theirs being likely to prevail, they refigned their caufe to him whofe power can controul all events. Wearied with their weaknefs and travelling, they made a ftop to recover themfelves, when the pilot returning, affured them they fhould foon receive fome provifions. The negroes were reduced fo low with hunger, that their behaviour was different from what it had been, conducting with more moderation. At their quarters in the evening, two white men came to them, one of which was a volunteer amongft the Britifh, the other had been taken a prifoner fome time before ; thefe two men brought fome hommony, and fugar made from the fweet maple, the fap being boiled to a confiftency, and is but a little inferior to the fugar imported from the iflands : of this provifion, and an hedge-hog which they found, they made a more comfortable fupper than they had enjoyed for many days.

15th. In the morning the volunteer having received information of the rough treatment the prifoners met with from the negroes, relieved them, by taking the four blacks under his care. It was not without much difficulty they croffed a large creek which was in their way, being obliged to fwim the horfes over it. Benjamin Gilbert began to fail ; the
Indian,

Indian, whofe property he was, highly irri-
tated at his want of ftrength, put a rope
about his neck, leading him along with it ;
fatigue at laft fo overcame him, that he fell
on the ground, when the Indian pulled the
rope fo hard, that he almoft choaked him :
his wife feeing this, refolutely interceded for
him, although the Indians bid her go forwards, as the others had gone on before
them ; this fhe refufed to comply with, unlefs her hufband might be permitted to accompany her ; they replied, " That they
" were determined to kill the old man,"
having before this fet him apart as a vic-
tim : but at length her intreaties prevailed,
and their hearts were turned from their cruel
purpofe. Had not an over-ruling providence
preferved him from their fury, he would in-
evitably have perifhed, as the Indians feldom
fhew mercy to thofe whom they devote to
death, which, as has been before obferved,
was the cafe with Benjamin Gilbert, whom
they had fmeared with black paint from this
motive. When their anger was a little moderated, they fet forwards to overtake the
reft of the company : their relations, who
had been eye-witneffes of the former part of
this fcene of cruelty, and expected they
would both have been murdered, rejoiced
greatly at their return, confidering their fafety
as a providential deliverance.

16th.

16th. Neceffity induced two of the Indians to fet off on horfeback, into the Seneca country, in fearch of provifions. The prifoners, in the mean time, were ordered to dig up a root, fomething refembling potatoes, which the Indians call whoppanies. They tarried at this place until towards the evening of the fucceeding day, and made a foup of wild onions and turnip-tops ; this they eat without bread or falt; it could not therefore afford fufficient fuftenance, either for young or old; their food being fo very light, their ftrength daily wafted.

17th. They left this place, and croffed the Genefee river, (which empties its waters into lake Ontario) on a raft of logs, bound together by hickory withes; this appeared to be a dangerous method of ferrying them over fuch a river, to thofe who had been unaccuftomed to fuch conveyances. They fixed their ftation near the Genefee banks, and procured more of the wild potatoe roots before-mentioned for their fupper.

18th. One of the Indians left the company, taking with him the fineft horfe they had, and in fome hours after returned with a large piece of meat, ordering the captives to boil it; this command they cheerfully performed, anxioufly watching the kettle, frefh meat being a rarity which they had not eat for a long time: the Indians, when it

was

was fufficiently boiled, diftributed to each one a piece, eating fparingly themfelves. The prifoners made their repaft without bread or falt, and eat with a good relifh, what they fuppofed to be frefh beef, but underftood it was horfe-flefh.

A fhrill halloo, which they heard, gave the prifoners fome uneafinefs ; one of the Indians immediately rode to examine the caufe, and found it was Capt. Rowland Monteur, and his brother John's wife, with fome other Indians, who were feeking them with provifion. The remainder of the company foon reached them, and they divided fome bread, which they had brought, into fmall pieces, according to the number of the company.

Here is a large extent of rich farming land, remarkable for its levelnefs and beautiful meadows. The country is fo flat, that there are no falls in the rivers, and the waters run flow and deep ; and whenever fhowers defcend, they continue a long time muddied.

The captain and his company had brought with them cakes of hommony, and Indian corn ; of this they made a good meal. He appeared pleafed to fee the prifoners, having been abfent from them feveral days, and ordered them all round to fhake hands with him. From him they received information refpecting Jofeph Gilbert and Thomas Peart, who were feparated from the others on the 4th inftant,

inftant, that they had arrived at the Indian fettlements, fome time, in fafety.

The company ftaid the night at this place. One of the Indians refufed to fuffer any of them to come near his fire, or converfe with the prifoner, who in the diftribution had fallen to him.

19th. Pounding hommony was this day's employment, the weather being warm made it a hard tafk; they boiled and prepared it for fupper, the Indians fetting down to eat firft, and when they had concluded their meal, they wiped the fpoon on the foal of their mockafoons, and then gave it to the captives: hunger alone could prevail on any one to eat after fuch filth and naftinefs.

20th. Elizabeth Gilbert, the mother, being obliged to ride alone, miffed the path, for which the Indians repeatedly ftruck her. Their route ftill continued through rich meadow. After wandering for a time out of the direct path, they came to an Indian town, and obtained the neceffary information to purfue their journey: the Indians ran out of their huts to fee the prifoners, and to partake of the plunder, but no part of it fuited them. Being directed to travel the path back again, for a fhort diftance, they did fo, and then ftruck into another, and went on until night, by which time they were very hungry, not having eat fince morning; the kettle was

B   again

again set on the fire for hommony, this being their only food.

21st. The report of a morning-gun from Niagara, which they heard, contributed to raise their hopes, they rejoiced at being so near. An Indian was dispatched on horseback, to procure provisions from the fort.

Elizabeth Gilbert could not walk as fast as the rest, she was therefore sent forwards on foot, but was soon overtaken, and left behind, the rest being obliged by the Indians to go on without regarding her. She would have been greatly perplexed, when she came to a division-path, had not her husband lain a branch across the path which would have led her wrong: an affecting instance of both ingenuity and tenderness. She met several Indians, who passed by without speaking to her.

An Indian belonging to the company, who was on the horse Elizabeth Gilbert had rode, overtook her, and, as he went on slowly, conversing with her, endeavoured to alarm her, by saying, that she would be left behind, and perish in the woods; yet, notwithstanding this, his heart was so softened before he had gone any great distance from her, that he alighted from the horse and left him, that she might be able to reach the rest of the company. The more seriously she considered this, the more it appeared to her to be a
convincing

convincing inftance of the over-ruling protection of him, who can " turn the heart of man, as the hufbandman turneth the watercourfe in his field."

22d. As the Indians approached nearer their habitations, they frequently repeated their halloos, and after fome time, they received an anfwer in the fame manner, which alarmed the company much; but they foon difcovered it to proceed from a party of Whites and Indians, who were on fome expedition, though their pretence was, that they were for New-York. Not long after parting with thefe, the captain's wife came to them; fhe was daughter to Siangorochti, king of the Senecas, but her mother being a Cayuga, fhe was ranked among that nation, the children generally reckoning their defcent from the mother's fide. This princefs was attended by the captain's brother, John, one other Indian, and a white prifoner, who had been taken at Wyoming by Rowland Monteur; fhe was dreffed altogether in the Indian manner, fhining with gold lace and filver baubles: they brought with them from the fort a fupply of provifions. The captain being at a diftance behind, when his wife came, the company waited for him. After the cuftomary falutations, he addreffed himfelf to his wife, telling her that Rebecca was her daughter, and that fhe muft not be induced, by any

confideration,

confideration, to part with her; whereupon
fhe took a filver ring off her finger, and put
it upon Rebecca, by which fhe was adopted
as her daughter.

They feafted upon the provifions that were
brought, for they had been for feveral days
before pinched with hunger, what fuftenance
they could procure not being fufficient to
fupport nature.

23d. Their fpirits were in fome degree revived, by the enjoyment of plenty, added to
the pleafing hope of fome favourable event
procuring their releafement, as they were not
far diftant from Niagara.

The Indians proceeded on their journey,
and continued whooping in the moft frightful
manner. In this day's route they met another company of Indians, who compelled Benjamin Gilbert, the elder, to fit on the ground,
and put feveral queftions to him, to which
he gave them the beft anfwers he could; they
then took his hat from him, and went off.

Going through a fmall town, near Niagara,
an Indian woman came out of one of the
huts, and ftruck each of the captives a blow.
Not long after their departure from this place,
Jeffe, Rebecca, and their mother, were detained until the others had got out of their
fight, when the mother was ordered to pufh
on; and as fhe had to go by herfelf, fhe was
much perplexed what courfe to take, as there

was

vas no path by which fhe could be directed:
n this dilemma, fhe concluded to keep as
ftraight forward as poffible, and after fome
fpace of time, fhe had the fatisfaction of
)vertaking the others. The pilot then made
ι fhort ftay, that thofe who were behind
might come up, and the captain handed fome
·um round, giving each a dram, except the
:wo old folks, whom they did not confider
worthy of this notice. Here the captain,
who had the chief direction, painted Abner,
Jeffe, Rebecca, and Elizabeth Gilbert, jun.
and prefented each with a belt of wampum,
as a token of their being received into favour,
although they took from them all their hats
and bonnets, except Rebecca's.

  The prifoners were releafed from the heavy
loads they had heretofore been compelled to
carry, and was it not for the treatment they
expected on their approaching the Indian
towns, and the hardfhip of a feparation,
their fituation would have been tolerable;
but the horror of their minds, arifing from
the dreadful yells of the Indians, as they approached the hamlets, is eafier conceived
than defcribed, for they were no ftrangers to
the cuftomary cruelty exercifed upon captives on entering their towns : the Indians,
men, women, and children, collect together,
bringing clubs and ftones, in order to beat
them, which they ufually do with great feverity,

rity, by way of revenge for their relations who have been flain; this is performed immediately upon their entering the village where the warriors refide: this treatment cannot be avoided, and the blows, however cruel, muft be borne without complaint, and the prifoners are forely beaten, until their enemies are wearied with the cruel fport. Their fufferings were in this cafe very great, they received feveral wounds, and two of the women, who were on horfeback, were much bruifed by falling from their horfes, which were frightened by the Indians. Elizabeth, the mother, took fhelter by the fide of one of them, but upon his obferving that fhe met with fome favour upon his account, he fent her away; fhe then received feveral violent blows, fo that fhe was almoft difabled. The blood trickled from their heads in a ftream, their hair being cropt clofe, and the cloaths they had on, in rags, made their fituation truly piteous: whilft they were inflicting this revenge upon the captives, the king came, and put a ftop to any further cruelty, by telling them, " It was fufficient," which they immediately attended to.

Benjamin Gilbert, and Elizabeth his wife, Jeffe Gilbert, and his wife, were ordered to Captain Rowland Monteur's houfe; the women belonging to it were kind to them, and gave them fomething to eat: Sarah Gilbert,

Jeffe's

Jeſſe's wife, was taken from them by three women, in order to be placed in the family ſhe was to be adopted by.

Two officers from Niagara Fort, Captains Dace and Powel, came to ſee the priſoners, and prevent (as they were informed) any abuſe that might be given them: Benjamin Gilbert informed theſe officers, that he was apprehenſive they were in great danger of being murdered, upon which they promiſed him they would ſend a boat the next day, to bring them to Niagara.

24th. Notwithſtanding the kind intention of the officers, they did not derive the expected advantage from it, for the Indians inſiſted on their going to the fort on foot, although the bruiſes they had received the day before, from the many ſevere blows given them, rendered their journey on foot very diſtreſſing; but Captain Monteur obſtinately perſiſting, they dared not long remonſtrate, or refuſe.

When they left the Indian town, ſeveral iſſued from their huts after them, with ſticks in their hands, yelling and ſcreeching in a moſt diſmal manner; but through the interpoſition of four Indian women, who had come with the captives, to prevent any further abuſe they might receive, they were preſerved: one of them walking between Benjamin Gilbert and his wife, led them,

and

and defired Jeffe to keep as near them as he could; the other three walked behind, and prevailed with the young Indians to defift. They had not purfued their route long, before they faw Captain John Powel, who came from his boat, and perfuaded (though with fome difficulty) the Indians to get into it, with the captives, which relieved them from the apprehenfions of further danger. After reaching the fort, Captain Powel introduced them to Col. Guy Johnfon, and Col. Butler, who afked the prifoners many queftions, in the prefence of the Indians. They prefented the Captain with a belt of wampum, which is a conftant practice among them, when they intend a ratification of the peace. Before their connexion with Europeans, thefe belts were made of fhells, found on the coafts of New-England and Virginia, which were fawed out into beads of an oblong fhape, about a quarter of an inch long, which, when ftrung together on leathern ftrings, and thefe ftrings faftened with fine threads made of finews, compofe what is called a belt of wampum: but fince the whites have gained footing among them, they make ufe of the common glafs beads for this purpofe.

The Indians, according to their ufual cuftom and ceremony, at three feparate times, ordered the prifoners to fhake hands with Col. Johnfon.

25th.

25th. Benjamin Gilbert, Elizabeth his wife, and Jeffe Gilbert, were furrendered to Col. Johnfon: this deliverance from fuch fcenes of diftrefs, as they had become acquainted with, gave them a more free opportunity of clofe reflection than heretofore.

The many forrowful days and nights they had paffed, the painful anxiety attendant on their frequent feparation from each other, and the uncertainty of the fate of the reft of their family, overwhelmed them with grief.

26th. Expreffion is too weak to defcribe their diftrefs, on leaving their children with thefe hard mafters; they were not unacquainted with many of the difficulties, to which they would neceffarily be expofed in a refidence amongft Indians, and the lofs which the young people would fuftain, for want of a civilized and Chriftian education.

27th. In this defponding fituation, the kindnefs of fympathy was awakened in one of the Indian women, who even forgot her prejudices, and wiped away the tears which trickled down Elizabeth Gilbert's cheeks.

The particular attention of Col. Johnfon's houfekeeper to them, from a commiferation of their diftrefs, claims their remembrance: Benjamin, his wife, and Jeffe Gilbert, were invited to her houfe, where fhe not only gave the old folks her beft room, but administered

B 5   miniftered

miniftered to their neceffities, and endeavoured to footh their forrows.

Jeffe Gilbert was favoured to get employ,
which, as it was fome alleviation of his
misfortunes, may be confidered as a providential kindnefs.

28th. A few days after they came to the
fort, they had information that Benjamin
Peart was by the river fide with the Indians;
upon hearing this report, his mother went
to fee him, but every attempt for his releafe was in vain, the Indians would by no
means give him up. From this place they
intended to march with their prifoner to the
Genefee River, about an hundred miles diftance. As the affectionate mother's folicita-
tions proved fruitlefs, her fon not only felt
the afflicting lofs of his wife and child, from
whom he had been torn fome time before,
but a renewal of his grief, on this fhort fight
of his parent: fhe procured him a hat, and
alfo fome falt, which was an acceptable bur-
den for the journey.

Benjamin Gilbert, converfing with the Indian captain who made them captives, obferved that he might fay what none of the other
Indians could, " That he had brought in the
" oldeft man, and the youngeft child;" his
reply to this was expreffive; " It was not I,
" but the great God who brought you
" through, for we were determined to kill
" you, but were prevented."

The

The Britiſh officers being acquainted that Jeſſe Gilbert's wife was among the Indians, with great tenderneſs agreed to ſeek her out, and after a diligent inquiry, found that ſhe was among the Delawares; they went to them, and endeavoured to agree upon terms for her releaſement; the Indians brought her to the fort the next day, but would not give her up to her relations.

29th. As the cabins of the Indians were but two miles from the fort, they went thither, and Jeſſe and the officers uſed every argument in their power to prevail upon them, repreſenting how hard it was to part theſe two young people; at length they conſented to bring her in next day, with their whole tribe, for a final releaſe.

30th. They accordingly came, but ſtarted ſo many objections, that ſhe was obliged to return with them.

31ſt. Early next morning Capt. Robeſon generouſly undertook to procure her liberty, which, after much attention and ſolicitude, he, together with Lieutenant Hillyard, happily accompliſhed. They gave the Indians ſeveral ſmall preſents, and gave them thirty pounds as a ranſom.

When Sarah Gilbert had obtained her liberty, ſhe altered her dreſs more in character for her ſex, than ſhe had been able to do whilſt amongſt the Indians, and went to her

huſbànd

husband and parents at Col. Johnson's, where she was joyfully received.

Col. Johnson's housekeeper continued her kind attentions to them, during their stay here, and procured clothing for them from the king's stores.

6th Month, 1st. About this time the Senecas, among whom Elizabeth Peart was captive, brought her with them to the fort; as soon as the mother heard of it, she went to her, and had some conversation with her, but could not learn where she was to be sent to; she then inquired of the interpreter, and pressed on his friendship, to learn what was to become of her daughter; this request he complied with, and informed her that she was to be given away to another family of the Senecas, and adopted among them, in the place of a deceased relation. Capt. Powel interested himself in her case likewise, and offered to purchase her of them, but the Indians refused to give her up; and as the mother and daughter expected they should see each other no more, their parting was very affecting.

The Indian woman who had adopted Rebecca as her daughter, came also to the fort, and Elizabeth Gilbert made use of this opportunity to inquire concerning her daughter; the interpreter informed her, there was no probability of obtaining the enlargement of her child, as the Indians would not part
with

with her: all she could do, was, to recom-
mend her to their notice, as very weakly, and
of confequence not able to endure much
fatigue.

2d. and 3d. Not many days after their arrival at Niagara, a veffel came up Lake Ontario to the fort, with orders for the prifoners
to go to Montreal. In this veffel came one
Capt. Brant, an Indian chief, high in rank
amongft them. Elizabeth Gilbert immediately applied herfelf to folicit and intereft
him on behalf of her children, who yet remained in captivity; he readily promifed her
to ufe his endeavours to procure their liberty.
A fhort time before they failed for Montreal,
they received accounts of Abner and Elizabeth Gilbert the younger, but it was alfo underftood that their poffeffors were not difpofed to give them up. As the profpect of
obtaining the releafe of their children was
fo very difcouraging, it was no alleviation to
their diftrefs, to be removed to Montreal,
where, in all probability, they would feldom
be able to gain any information refpecting
them; on which account they were very foli-
citous to ftay at Niagara, but the Colonel faid
they could not remain there, unlefs the fon
would enter into the king's fervice; this
could not be confented to, therefore they
chofe to fubmit to every calamity which
might be permitted to befal them, and con-
fide in the great controller of events.

Here

Here they became acquainted with one Jesse Pawling, from Pennsylvania, who was an officer among the British, and behaved with kindness and respect to the prisoners, which induced them to request his attention also to that part of the family remaining in captivity; it appeared to them of some consequence to gain an additional friend. The Colonel also gave his promise to exert himself on their behalf.

After continuing ten days at Col. Johnson's, they took boat in the forenoon of the 2d, being the 6th day of the week, and crossed the river Niagara, in-order to go on board the vessel, which lay in Lake Ontario, for Montreal. The officers procured necessaries for their voyage in great plenty, and they were also furnished with orders to draw more at certain places, as they might have occasion: these civilities may appear to many to be too trivial to be mentioned in this narrative; but those who have been in equal distress, will not be insensible of their value.

4th. The vessel sailed down the Lake on the sixth day of the week, and on first-day following, being the fourth day of the sixth month, 1780, came to Carlton Island, where there were such a number of small boats, which brought provisions, that it had the appearance of a fleet. Benjamin Gilbert and Jesse went on shore to obtain leave from the

the commanding officer to go to Montreal in the fmall boats, as the veffel they came in could proceed no further: they met with a kind reception, and their requeft was granted.

5th. On fecond day following, they left Carlton Ifland, which lies at the mouth of Lake Ontario, and took their paffage in open boats down the river St. Laurence, and paffed a number of fmall iflands. There is a rapid defcent in the waters of this river, which appears dangerous to thofe unacquainted with thefe kind of falls. The Frenchmen, who rowed the boats, kept them near the fhore, and paffed without much difficulty between the rocks.

6th, 7th, and 8th. Benjamin Gilbert had been much indifpofed before they left the fort, and his diforder was increafed by a rain which fell on their paffage, as they were without any covering. They paffed Ofwagatchy, an Englifh garrifon, by the fide of the river, but they were not permitted to ftop here; they proceeded down the St. Laurence, and the rain continuing, went on fhore on an ifland, in order to fecure themfelves from the weather: here they made a fhelter for Benjamin Gilbert, and when the rain ceafed, a place was prepared for him in the boat, that he might lie down with more eafe. His bodily weaknefs made fuch rapid progrefs, that

it

it rendered all the care and attention of his wife neceſſary, and likewiſe called forth all her fortitude; ſhe ſupported him in her arms, affording every poſſible relief to mitigate his extreme pains: and although in this diſtreſſed condition, he, notwithſtanding, gave a ſatisfactory evidence of the virtue and power of a patient and holy reſignation, which can diſarm the king of terrors, and receive him as a welcome meſſenger. Thus prepared, he paſſed from this ſtate of probation, the eighth day of the ſixth month, 1780, in the evening, leaving his wife and two children, who were with him, in all the anxiety of deep diſtreſs, although they had no doubt, but that their loſs was his everlaſting gain. Being without a light in the boat, the darkneſs of the night added not a little to their melancholy ſituation. As there were not any others with Elizabeth Gilbert but her children, and the four Frenchmen who managed the boat, and her apprehenſions alarmed her, leſt they ſhould throw the corpſe overboard, as they appeared to be an unfeeling company; ſhe therefore applied to ſome Britiſh officers who were in a boat behind them, who diſpelled her fears, and received her under their protection.

9th. In the morning they paſſed the garriſon of Coeur de Lac, and waited for ſome conſiderable time a ſmall diſtance below it.

'Squire

'Squire Campbell, who had the charge of the prisoners, when he heard of Benjamin Gilbert's decease, sent Jesse to the commandant of this garrison to get a coffin, in which they put the corpse, and very hastily interred him under an oak nor far from the fort. The boat-men would not allow his widow to pay the last tribute to his memory, but, regardless of her affliction, refused to wait; her distress on this occasion was great indeed, but being sensible that it was her duty to submit to the dispensations of an over-ruling providence, which are all ordered in wisdom, she endeavoured to support herself under her afflictions, and proceeded with the boat-men.

Near this place they passed by a grist-mill, which is maintained by a stone wing extended into the river St. Laurence; the stream being very rapid, acquires a force sufficient to turn the wheel, without the further expence of a dam.

The current carried their boat forwards with amazing rapidity, and the falls became so dangerous, that the boats could proceed no further; they therefore landed in the evening, and went to the commanding officer of fort Lasheen to request a lodging, but the houses in the garrison were so crowded, that it was with difficulty they obtained a small room belonging to the boat-builders to retire to, and here they stowed themselves with ten others.

10th. The

10th. The garrifon of Lasheen is on the isle of Jesu, on which the town of Montreal stands, about the distance of nine miles; hither our travellers had to go by land, and as they were entirely unacquainted with the road, they took the advantage of an empty cart (which was going to the town) for the women to ride in.

The land in this neighbourhood is very stoney, and the foil thin; the cattle small, and ill-favoured.

When they arrived at Montreal, they were introduced to Brigadier General M'Clean, who after examining them, fent them to one Duquefne, an officer amongft the loyalifts, who being from home, they were defired to wait in the yard until he came; this want of politenefs gave them no favourable impreffions of the mafter of the houfe; when he returned he read their pafs, and gave Jeffe an order for three days provifions.

Daniel M'Ulphin received them into his houfe; by him they were treated with great kindnefs, and the women continued at his houfe, and worked five weeks for him.

Jeffe Gilbert met with employ at Thomas Bufby's, where he lived very agreeably for the fpace of nine months.

Elizabeth Gilbert had the fatisfaction of an eafy employ at Adam Scott's, merchant, having the fuperintendance of his kitchen; but
about

about fix weeks after she engaged in his fervice, Jeffe's wife Sarah was taken fick at Thomas Bufby's, which made it neceffary for her mother to difengage herfelf from the place where she was fo agreeably fituated, in order to nurfe her. Thefe three were favoured to be confidered as the king's prifoners, having rations allowed them; this affiftance was very comfortable; but Elizabeth's name being erafed out of the lift at a time when they needed an additional fupply, they were much ftraightened: upon an application to one Col. Campbell, he, together with 'Squire Campbell, took down a fhort account of her fufferings and fituation, and after preparing a concife narrative, they applied to the Brigadier General, to forward it to General Haldimand at Quebec, defiring his attention to the fufferers, who fpeedily iffued his orders that the releafement of the family fhould be procured, with particular injunctions for every garrifon to furnifh them with neceffaries as they came down.

As foon as Sarah Gilbert recovered from her indifpofition, her mother returned to Adam Scott's family.

Thomas Gomerfom hearing of their fituation, came to fee them; he was educated a Quaker, and had been a merchant of New-York, and travelled with Robert Walker in his religious vifits; but, upon the commencement

ment of the war, had deviated from his former principles, and had loft all the appearance of a friend, wearing a fword: he behaved with refpect to the prifoners, and made Elizabeth a prefent.

The particular attention of Col. Clofs, and the care he fhewed by writing to Niagara, on behalf of the captives, as he was entirely a ftranger to her, is remembered with gratitude.

As there was an opportunity of hearing from Niagara, it gave them great pleafure to be informed that Elizabeth Gilbert was amongft the white people, fhe having obtained her releafe from the Indians, prior to the others.

Sarah Gilbert, wife of Jeffe, becoming a mother, Elizabeth left the fervice fhe was engaged in, Jeffe having taken a houfe, that fhe might give her daughter every neceffary attendance; and in order to make their fituation as comfortable as poffible, they took a child to nurfe, which added a little to their income. After this, Elizabeth Gilbert hired herfelf to iron a day for Adam Scott; whilft fhe was at her work, a little girl belonging to the houfe, acquainted her that there were fome who wanted to fee her, and, upon entering into the room, fhe found fix of her children; the joy and furprife fhe felt on this occafion were beyond what we fhall attempt

attempt to defcribe. A meffenger was fent
to inform Jeffe and his wife, that Jofeph Gilbert, Benjamin Peart, Elizabeth his wife,
and young child, Abner and Elizabeth Gilbert the younger, were with their mother.
It muft afford very pleafing reflections to any
affectionate difpofition, to dwell a while on
this fcene, that after a captivity of upwards
of fourteen months, fo happy a meeting
fhould take place.

Thomas Peart, who had obtained his liberty, and tarried at Niagara, that he might
be of fervice to the two yet remaining in
captivity, viz. Benjamin Gilbert, jun. and
Rebecca Gilbert.

Abigail Dodfon, the daughter of a neigh-
bouring farmer, who was taken with them,
having inadvertently informed the Indians
fhe was not of the Gilbert family, all at-
tempts for her liberty were fruitlefs.

We fhall now proceed to relate how Jofeph
Gilbert, the eldeft fon of the deceafed, fared
amongft the Indians: he, with Thomas
Peart, Benjamin Gilbert, jun. and Jeffe Gilbert's wife Sarah, were taken along the Weftward Path, as before related; after fome fhort
continuance in this path, Thomas Peart and
Jofeph Gilbert were taken from the other
two, and by a different route, through many
difficulties, they were brought to Caracadera,
where they received the infults of the women
and

and children, whofe hufbands or parents had fallen in their hoftile excurfions.

Jofeph Gilbert was feparated from his companion, and removed to an Indian villa, called Nundow, about feven miles from Caracadera; his refidence was, for feveral weeks, in the king's family, whofe hamlet was fuperior to the other fmall huts. The king himfelf brought him fome hommony, and treated him with great civility, intending his adoption into the family, in the place of one of his fons, who was flain when General Sullivan drove them from their habitations. As Nundow was not to be the place of his abode, his quarters were foon changed, and he was taken back to Caracadera; but his weaknefs of body was fo great, that he was two days accomplifhing this journey, which was only feven miles, and not able to procure any other food than roots and herbs, the Indian oeconomy leaving them without any provifions to fubfift on. Here they adopted him into the family of one of the king's fons, informing him, that if he would marry amongft them, he fhould enjoy the privileges which they enjoyed; but this propofal he was not difpofed to comply with; and as he was not over anxious to conceal his diflike to them, the fufferings he underwent were not alleviated. The manner of his life differing fo much from what he had

before

before been accuftomed to, having to eat the
wild roots and herbs before-mentioned, and
as he had been lame from a child, and fubject to frequent indifpofitions, it was requifite
for him to pay more attention to his weak
habit of body, than his captors were willing
he fhould. When the mafter of the family
was at home, the refpect he fhewed to Jofeph,
and his kindnefs to him, rendered his fituation more tolerable than in his abfence.
Frequently fuffering with hunger, the privi-
lege of a plenteous table appeared to him
as an ineftimable bleffing, which claimed the
warmeft devotion of gratitude : in fuch a
diftreffed fituation, the hours rolled over with
a tedioufnefs almoft infupportable, as he had
no agreeable employ to relieve his mind from
the reflections of his forrowful captivity :
this manner of life continued about three
months, and when they could no longer procure a fupply by their hunting, neceffity
compelled them to go to Niagara Fort for
provifion. The greater number of the Indians belonging to Caracadera attended on
this journey, in order to obtain a fupply of
provifions; their want of oeconomy being fo
great, as to have confumed fo early as the
eighth month all they had raifed the laft
year, and the prefent crops unfit to gather:
their profufe manner of ufing their fcant pittance of provifion, generally introducing a
famine,

famine, after a fhort time of feafting. They compute the diftance from Caracadera, to Niagara fort, to be of 130 miles; on this journey they were upwards of five days, taking fome venifon in their route, and feafting with great greedinefs, as they had been a long time without meat.

When they reached the fort, they procured clothing from the king's ftores for Jofeph Gilbert, fuch as the Indians ufually wear themfelves, a match-coat, leggings, &c. His indifpofition confined him at Col. Johnfon's for feveral days, during which time the Britifh officers endeavoured to agree with the Indians for his releafement, but they would not confent. The afflicting account of the death of his father, which was here communicated to him, fpread an additional gloom on his mind. After continuing at the fort about four weeks, the Indians ordered him back with them; this was a fore ftroke, to leave a degree of eafe and plenty, and refume the hardfhips of an Indian life: with this uncomfortable profpect before him, added to his lamenefs, the journey was toilfome and painful. They were five days in their return, and when they arrived, their corn was ripe for ufe; this, with the advantage of hunting, as the game was in its greateft perfection, furnifhed a prefent comfortable fubfiftence.

Jofeph

Jofeph had permiffion to vifit his fellow captive, Thomas Peart, who was at a fmall town of the Indians, about feven miles diftance, called Nundow, to whom he communicated the forrowful intelligence of their mother's widowed fituation.

At the firft approach of fpring, Jofeph Gilbert and his adopted brother employed themfelves in procuring rails, and repairing the fence about the lot of ground they intended to plant with corn; as this part of preferving the grain was allotted to them, the planting and culture was affigned to the women, their hufbandry being altogether performed by the hoe.

The Indian manner of life was by no means agreeable to Jofeph Gilbert; their irregularity in their meals was hard for him to bear; when they had provifions in plenty, they obferved no plan of domeftic oeconomy, but indulged their voracious appetites, which foon confumed their ftock, and a famine fucceeded.

In the early part of the fixth month, 1781, their corn was fpent, and they were obliged to have recourfe again to the wild herbage and roots, and were fo reduced for want of provifion, that the Indians having found the carcafe of a dead horfe, they took the meat and roafted it.

An officer from the fort came down to inquire into the fituation of the Indians, upon

C   obferving

observing the low condition Joseph was in, not being likely to continue long without some relief, which the officer privately afforded, he being permitted to frequent his house, he advised him by flight to endeavour an escape from the Indians, informing him that he had no other expedient for his release; this confirmed him in a resolution he had for some time been contemplating, but his lameness and weak habit, for want of proper sustenance, rendered it impracticable to make such an attempt at that time, and it would require much care and attention to his own health and strength, to gather sufficient for such an undertaking; he therefore made use of the liberty allowed him to visit the officer, and partake of his kindness and assistance, that he might be prepared for the journey.

Embracing a favourable opportunity, when the men were generally from home, some in their war expeditions, and some out hunting, he left them one night whilst the family slept, and made the best of his way towards Niagara fort, following the path, as he had once before gone along it. Having a small piece of bread which he took from the hut, he made a hasty repast, travelling day and night, in order to escape from the further distresses of captivity. As he neither took any sleep, or other food by the way than the

piece

piece of bread mentioned, for the two days and nights he purfued his journey, he was much fatigued when he reached the fort, and he experienced the effects for feveral days. Upon his applying to Col. Johnfon, he was hofpitably entertained, and the next day faw three of the Indians whom he had left at the town when he fet off.

After a few days ftay here, as moft of the family were difcharged from captivity, and waiting for a paffage to Montreal, a veffel was fitted to take them on board, in order to proceed down the lake.

We come next to Benjamin Peart, who remained the firft night after his arriving at the Indian huts, with his wife and child, but was feparated from them the next day, and taken about a mile and an half, and pre-fented to one of the families of the Seneca nation, and afterwards introduced to one of their chiefs, who made a long harangue, which Benjamin did not underftand. The Indians then gave him to a Squaw, in order to be received as her adopted child, who ordered him to a private hut, where the women wept over him in remembrance of the relation in whofe ftead he was received: after this he went with his mother (by adop-tion) to Niagara river, about two miles below the great falls, and ftaid here feveral days, then went to the fort on their way to

the

the Genefee River, where he had the pleafure
of converfing with his mother, and receiving
information concerning his wife and child;
but even this fatisfaction was fhort-lived,
for he neither could obtain permiffion to vifit
his wife, nor was he allowed to converfe free-
ly with his mother, as the Indians hurried
him on board their bark canoes, where having placed their provifions, they proceeded
with expedition down the Lake to the mouth
of the Genefee River; the computed diftance from the fmall village to the mouth
of the river being one hundred miles, and
from thence up the Genefee to the place of
their deftination, thirty miles; in their paffage up the river they were about five days,
and as the falls in this river near its entrance
into Lake Ontario has made a carrying-
place of about two miles, they dragged
their canoe this diftance to the place of boat-
ing above the falls. There were nine Indians of the party with them. They frequently caught fifh by the way.

It no doubt was a fore affliction to Benjamin to be fo far removed from his wife and
child whilft among the Indians: patience
and refignation alone could endure it.

When the party arrived at the place of
their defigned fettlement, they foon erected
a fmall hut or wigwam, and the ground
being rich and level, they began with their
plan-

plantation of Indian corn. Two white men who had been taken prisoners, the one from Sufquehanna, the other from Minifinks, both in Pennfylvania, lived near his new fettlement, and were allowed by the Indians to ufe the horfes, and plant for themfelves. Thefe men lightened the toil of Benjamin Peart's fervitude, as he was frequently in their company, and he had the liberty of doing fomething for himfelf, though without much fuccefs.

His new habitation, as it was not very healthy, introduced frefh difficulties, for he had not continued here long, before he was afflicted with ficknefs, which preyed upon him near three months, the Indians repeatedly endeavouring to relieve him by their knowledge in fimples, but their endeavours proved ineffectual; the approach of the winter feafon afforded the relief fought for. Their provifion was not very tempting to a weakly conftitution, having nothing elfe than hommony, and but fhort allowance even of that, infomuch that when his appetite increafed, he could not procure food fufficient to recruit his ftrength. The company of his brother Thomas Peart, who vifited him, was a great comfort, and as the town he lived at was but the diftance of eighteen miles, they had frequent opportunities of condoling with each other in their diftrefs.

The

The Indian men being abfent on one of their war excurfions, and the women employed in gathering the corn, left Benjamin Peart much leifure to reflect in folitude.

Towards the beginning of the winter feafon the men returned, and built themfelves a log houfe for a granary, and then removed about twenty miles from their fettlement into the hunting country, and procured a great variety of game, which they ufually eat without bread or falt. As he had been with the Indians for feveral months, their language became more familiar to him.

Hunting and feafting after their manner being their only employ, they foon cleared the place where they fettled of the game, which made a fecond removal neceffary, and they are fo accuftomed to this wandering life, that it becomes their choice.

They fixed up a log hut in this fecond hunting-place, and continued until the fecond month, when they returned to their firft fettlement, though their ftay was but a few days, and then back again to their log hut.

A heavy rain falling melted fome of the fnow, which had covered the ground about two feet deep.

The whole family concluded upon a journey to Niagara Fort by land, which was completed in feven days. At the fort he had the fatisfaction of converfing with his brother
ther

ther Thomas Peart, and the fame day his
wife alfo came from Buffalo Creek, with the
Senecas to the fort; this happy meeting,
after an abfence of ten months, drew tears
of joy from them. He made an inquiry
after his child, as he had neither heard from
it or the mother fince their feparation. The
Indians not approving of their converfing
much together, as they imagined they would
remember their former fituation, and become
lefs contented with their prefent manner of
life, they feparated them again the fame day,
and took Benjamin's wife about four miles
diftance; but the party with whom he came,
permitted him to ftay here feveral nights;
and when the Indians had completed their
purpofe of traffick, they returned, taking
him fome miles back with them to one of
their towns; but upon his telling them he
was defirous of returning to the fort to procure fomething he had before forgot, in
order for his journey, he was permitted. As
he ftaid the night, his adopted brother the
Indian came for him; but upon his complaining that he was fo lame as to prevent
his travelling with them, they fuffered him
to remain behind.

He continued at the fort about two months
before the Indians came back again, and as
he laboured for the white people, he had an
opportunity of procuring falt provifion from

the

the king's stores, which had been for a long time a dainty to him.

When one of the Indians (a second adopted brother) came for him, Benjamin went with him to Capt. Powel, who with earnest solicitations, and some presents, prevailed upon the Indian to suffer him to stay until he returned from his war expedition; but this was the last he ever made, as he lost his life on the frontiers of New-York.

After this another Captain (a third adopted brother) came to the fort, and when Benjamin Peart saw him, he applied to Adjutant Gen. Wilkinson to intercede for his release, who accordingly waited upon Col. Johnson and other officers, to prevail with them to exert themselves on his behalf; they concluded to hold a council with the Indians for this purpose, who, after some deliberation, surrendered him up to Col. Johnson, for which he gave them a valuable compensation.

Benjamin Peart, after his release, was employed in Col. Johnson's service, and continued with him for several months. His child had been released for some time, and his wife, by earnest intreaty and plea of sickness, had prevailed with the Indians to permit her to stay at the fort, which proved a great consolation and comfort after so long a separation.

About

About the middle of the eighth month there was preparation made for their proceeding to Montreal, as by this time there were fix of the prifoners ready to go in a fhip which lay in Lake Ontario, whofe names were Jofeph Gilbert, Benjamin Peart, his wife and child, Abner Gilbert, and Elizabeth Gilbert the younger. Thefe went on board the veffel to Charlton Ifland, which is as far as the large veffels they ufe in the lake can proceed; the remainder of the way (on account of the frequent fhoals) they are obliged to go in fmaller boats.

The commanding officer at Niagara procured a fuitable fupply of provifions, and furnifhed them with orders to draw more at the feveral garrifons, as occafion required.

In two days they arrived at the upper end of Charlton Ifland, and went to the commander in chief to fhew their pafs, and obtain what they were in need of. Afterwards they continued on to the garrifon of Ofwagotchy, by the fide of the river St. Laurence, in an open boat rowed by four Frenchmen, this clafs of people being chiefly employed in laborious fervices.

The ftream was fo rapid, and full of rocks, that the prifoners were too much alarmed to remain in the boat, and concluded to go on fhore until they paffed the danger; but the Frenchmen, who had been accuftomed to

thefe

thefe wild and violent rapids (the longeft of which is known by the name of the long Sou) kept on board. This furprifing fcene continued for the diftance of fix miles, and they viewed it with a degree of horror, their heads becoming almoft giddy with the profpect. When the boats had fhot the falls, they again went on board, and continued down the river to Cour de Lac. No great diftance below this they ancnored, and landed at the place where their father was interred, fhedding many tears of filial affection to his memory. They afterwards applied to the commanding officer of the garrifon for provifions and other neceffaries; they then bid adieu to this folemn fpot of forrow, and proceeded to Lafheen, which they reached the twenty-fourth day of the eighth month, having been eight days on their voyage.

After refrefhing themfelves at this garrifon, they fet forward on foot for Montreal, which they reached the fame day. They went to the Brigadier General, and fhewed him their paffport, and as foon as at liberty, waited on their mother at Adam Scott's, as has been already related.

The fituation of Elizabeth Peart, wife of Benjamin, and her child, is next to be related.

After fhe and the child were parted from her hufband, Abigail Dodfon and the child

were

were taken several miles in the night to a little hut, where they ftaid till morning, and the day following were taken within eight miles of Niagara, where fhe was adopted into one of the families of Senecas; the ceremony of adoption to her was tedious and diftreffing; they obliged her to fit down with a young man an Indian, and the eldeft chieftain of the family repeating a jargon of words to her unintelligible, but which fhe confidered as fome form amongft them of marriage, and this apprehenfion introduced the moft violent agitations, as fhe was determined, at all events, to oppofe any ftep of this nature; but after the old Indian concluded his fpeech, fhe was relieved from the dreadful embarraffment fhe had been under, as fhe was led away by another Indian.

Abigail Dodfon was given the fame day to one of the families of the Cayuga nation, fo that Elizabeth Peart faw her no more.

The man who led Elizabeth from the company took her into the family for whom they adopted her, and introduced her to her parents, brothers, and fifters, in the Indian ftile, who received her very kindly, and made a grievous lamentation over her according to cuftom. After fhe had been with them two days, the whole family left their habitation, and went about two miles to Fort Slufher, where they ftaid feveral days.

This

This fort is about one mile above Niagara Falls.

As she was much indifpofed, the Indians were detained feveral days for her; but as they cared little for her, fhe was obliged to lie on the damp ground, which prevented her fpeedy recovery. As foon as her diforder abated of its violence, they fet off in a bark canoe which they had provided, intending for Buffalo Creek; and as they went flowly, they had an opportunity of taking fome fifh.

When they arrived at the place of their intended fettlement, they went on fhore, and built an houfe.

A few days after they came to this new fettlement, they returned with Elizabeth to Fort Slufher, when fhe was told her child muft be taken away from her; this was truly afflicting, but all remonftrances were in vain.

From Fort Slufher fhe travelled on foot, carrying her child to Niagara, it being eighteen miles, and in fultry weather, rendered it a painful addition to the thoughts of parting with her tender offspring. The intent of their journey was to obtain provifions, and their ftay at the fort was of feveral days continuance. Capt. Powel afforded her an afylum in his houfe.

The Indians took the child from her, and went with it acrofs the river to adopt it into
the

the family they had affigned for it, notwithftanding Capt. Powel, at his wife's requeft,
interceded that it might not be removed
from its mother; but as it was fo young,
they returned it to the mother after its adoption, until it fhould be convenient to fend
it to the family under whofe protection it
was to be placed.

Obtaining the provifion and other neceffaries they came to Niagara to trade for, they
returned to Fort Slufher on foot, from whence
they embarked in their canoes. It being
near the time of planting, they ufed much
expedition in this journey.

The labour and drudgery in a family falling to the fhare of the women, Elizabeth had
to affift the Squaw in preparing the ground,
and planting corn.

Their provifion being fcant they fuffered
much, and as their dependance for a fufficient fupply until the gathering their crop,
was on what they fhould receive from the
fort, they were under the neceffity of making
a fecond journey thither.

They were two days on the road at this
time. A fmall diftance before they came to
the fort, they took her child from her, and
fent it to its deftined family, and it was feveral months before fhe had an opportunity of
feeing it again. After being taken from her
hufband, to lofe her darling infant, was a
fevere

severe stroke: she lamented her condition, and wept sorely, for which one of the Indians inhumanly struck her. Her Indian father seemed a little moved to behold her so distressed; and in order to console her, assured her they would bring it back again, but she saw it not until the spring following.

After they had disposed of their peltries; they returned to their habitation by the same route which they had come.

With a heart oppressed with sorrow, Elizabeth trod back her steps, mourning for her lost infant; for this idea presented itself continually to her mind; but as she experienced how fruitless, nay, how dangerous, solicitations in behalf of her child were, she dried up her tears, and pined in secret.

Soon after they reached their own habitation, Elizabeth Peart was again afflicted with sickness. At the first they shewed some attention to her complaints; but as she did not speedily recover so as to be able to work, they discontinued every attention, and built a small hut by the side of the corn-field, placing her in it to mind the corn. In this lonely condition she saw a white man, who had been made prisoner among the Indians: he informed her that her child was released, and with the white people; this information revived her drooping spirits, and a short time after she recovered of her indisposition, but her employment

employment ftill continued of attending the corn until it was ripe for gathering, which fhe affifted in. When the harveft was over, they permitted her to return, and live with them.

A time of plenty commenced, and they lived as if they had fufficient to laft the year through, faring plenteoufly every day.

A drunken Indian came to the cabin one day, and the old Indian woman complaining to him of Elizabeth, his behaviour exceedingly terrified her; he ftormed like a fury, and at length ftruck her a violent blow, which laid her on the ground; he then began to pull her about, and abufe her much, when another of the women interpofed, and refcued her from further fuffering: fuch is the fhocking effect of fpirituous liquor on thefe people; it totally deprives them both of fenfe and humanity.

A tedious winter prevented them from leaving their habitation, and deprived her of the pleafure of hearing often from her friends, who were very much fcattered; but a prifoner, who had lately feen her hufband, informed her of his being much indifpofed at the Genefee River, which was upwards of one hundred miles diftance: on receiving this intelligence, fhe ftood in need of much confolation, but had no fource of comfort, except in her own bofom.

Near

Near the return of spring their provision failing, they were compelled to go off to the fort for a fresh supply, having but a small portion of corn, which they allowanced out once a day.

Through snow and severe frost they went for Niagara, suffering much from the exceffive cold. And when they came within a few miles of the fort, which they were four days accomplishing, they struck up a small wigwam for some of the family with the prisoners to live in until the return of the warriors from the fort.

As soon as Capt. Powel's wife heard that the young child's mother had come with the Indians, she defired to see her, claiming some relationship in the Indian way, as she had also been a prisoner amongst them. They granted her request, and Elizabeth was accordingly introduced, and informed that her husband was returned to the fort, and there was some expectations of his releafe. The fame day Benjamin Peart came to see his wife, but could not be permitted to continue with her, as the Indians infisted on her going back with them to their cabin, which, as has been related, was fome miles diftant.

Elizabeth Peart was not allowed for fome days to go from the cabin, but a white family, who had bought her child from the Indians to whom it had been prefented, offered

fered the party with whom Elizabeth was confined a bottle of rum, if they would bring her acrofs the river to her child; which they did, and delighted the fond mother with this happy meeting, as fhe had not feen it for the fpace of eight months.

She was permitted to ftay with the family where her child was for two days, when fhe returned with the Indians to their cabin. After fome time fhe obtained a further permiffion to go to the fort, where fhe had fome needle work from the white people, which afforded her a plea for often vifiting it. At length Capt. Powel's wife prevailed with them to fuffer her to continue a few days at her houfe, and work for her family, which was granted. At the expiration of the time, upon the coming of the Indians for her to return with them, fhe pleaded indifpofition, and by this means they were repeatedly diffuaded from taking her with them.

As the time of planting drew nigh, fhe made ufe of a little addrefs to retard her departure; having a fmall fwelling on her neck, fhe applied a poultice, which led the Indians into a belief it was improper to remove her, and they confented to come again for her in two weeks.

Her child was given up to her foon after her arrival at the fort, where fhe lodged at Capt. Powell's, and her hufband came frequently

ly to vifit her, which was a great happinefs, as her trials in their feparation had been many.

At the time appointed fome of the Indians came again, but fhe ftill pleaded indifpofition, and had confined herfelf to her bed. One of the women interrogated her very clofely, but did not infift upon her going back. Thus feveral months elapfed, fhe contriving delays as often as they came.

When the veffel which was to take the other five, among whom were her hufband and child, was ready to fail, the officers at Niagara concluded fhe might alfo go with them, as they faw no reafonable objection, and they doubted not but it was in their power to fatisfy thofe Indians, who confidered her as their property.

Abner Gilbert, another of the captives, when the company had reached the Indian town within three miles of Niagara Fort, was, with Elizabeth Gilbert the younger, feparated from the reft, about the latter part of the 5th month 1780, and were both adopted into John Hufton's family, who was of the Cayuga nation. After a ftay of three days at or near the fettlement of thefe Indians, they removed to a place near the great falls, which is about eighteen miles diftant from the fort, and loitered here three days more; they then croffed the river, and fettled near its banks, clearing a piece of land, and prepared

pared it by the hoe for planting. Until they could gather their corn, their dependance was entirely upon the fort.

After the space of three weeks, they packed up their moveables, which they generally carry with them in their rambles, and went down the river to get provisions at Butlerfbury, a small village built by Col. Butler, and is on the opposite side of the river to Niagara Fort. They staid one night at the village, observing great caution that none of the white people should converse with the prisoners. Next day, after transacting their business, they returned to their settlement, and continued there but about one week, when it was concluded they must go again for Butlerfbury; after they had left their habitation a small distance, the head of the family met with his brother, and as they are very ceremonious in such interviews, the place of meeting was their rendezvous for the day and night. In the morning the family, with the brother before-mentioned, proceeded for Butlerfbury, and reached it before night. They went to the house of an Englishman, one John Secord, who was stiled brother to the chief of the family, having lived with him some time before.

After some deliberation, it was agreed that Elizabeth Gilbert should continue in this family till sent for; this was an agreeable change to her.

Abner

Abner returned with them to the fettle-ment, his employ being to fence and fecure the corn-patch; fometimes he had plenty of provifions, but was often in want.

The miftrefs of the family one day intend-ing for Butlerfbury, ordered Abner to pre-pare to go with her; but fhe had not gone far before fhe fent him back. Notwithftanding he had long been inured to frequent difap-pointments, he was much mortified at re-turning, as he expected to have feen his fifter. When the woman came home, fhe gave him no information about her, and all inquiries on his part would have been fruitlefs.

The place they had fettled at ferved for a dwelling until fall, and as it was not very far diftant from the fort, by often applying for provifion, they were not fo much dif-treffed between the failing of their old crop, and the gathering of the new one, as thofe who lived at a greater diftance.

In the fall John Hufton, the head of the family, went out hunting, and in his return caught cold from his carelefs manner of lying in the wet, and thereby loft the ufe of his limbs for a long time. On being informed of his fituation, the family moved to the place where he was; they fixed a fhelter over him, as he was unable to move himfelf, and conti-nued here about a month; but as it was re-mote from any fettlement, and they had to go often to the fort for the neceffaries of life, they

they concluded to return to their own habitation. Abner, one Indian man, and some of the women, carried the cripple in a blanket about two miles; this was so hard a task, they agreed to put up a small house, and wait for his recovery: But not long after they had an opportunity of conveying him on horseback to the landing, about nine miles above the fort. As this was their plantation, and the time of gathering their crops, they took in their corn, which, as has been before observed, is the business of the women. Then they changed their quarters, carrying the lame Indian as before in a blanket, down to the river side, when they went on board canoes, and crossed the river, in order to get to their hunting-ground, where they usually spend the winter.

Abner Gilbert lived a dronish Indian life, idle and poor, having no other employ than the gathering of hickory nuts; and although young, his situation was very irksome.

As soon as the family came to the hunting-ground, they patched up a slight hut for their residence, and employed themselves in hunting. They took Abner along with them in one of their tours, but they were then unsuccessful, taking nothing but rackoons and porcupines.

The crop of Indian corn proving too scant a pittance for the winter, Abner, on this account,

count had fome agreeable employ, which was to vifit the fort, and procure a fupply of provifions, which continued to be his employment for the remainder of the feafon.

In the fpring, John Hufton, the Indian who had been lame the whole winter, recovered, and unhappily had it in his power to obtain a fupply of rum, which he frequently drank to excefs; and always, when thus debauched, was extravagantly morofe, quarrelling with the women who were in the family, and at length left them. Soon after his departure, the family moved about 40 miles, near Buffalo Creek, which empties its waters into Lake Erie. At this place Abner heard of his fifter, Rebecca Gilbert, who ftill remained in captivity not far from his new habitation. This was their fummer refidence; they therefore undertook to clear a piece of land, in which they put corn, pumpkins and fquafhes.

Abner, having no ufeful employ, amufed himfelf with catching fifh in the lake, and furnifhed the family with frequent meffes of various kinds, which they eat without bread or falt; for the diftance of this fettlement from the fort prevented them from obtaining provifions fo frequently as neceffary. Capt. John Powel and Thomas Peart, (the latter had by this time obtained his releafe from the Indians) and feveral others, came among the Indian fettlements with provifion and hoes for them. The account of their coming

ing foon fpread amongſt the Indians. The chiefs of every tribe came, bringing with them as many little ſticks as there were perſons in their tribe, to exprefs the number, in order to obtain a juſt proportion of the proviſion to be diſtributed. They are faid to be unacquainted with any other power of explaining numbers, than by this ſimple hieroglyphic mode.

It was upwards of a year ſince Abner had been parted from his relations, and as he had not feen his brother Tho. Peart in that ſpace of time, this unexpected meeting gave him great joy, but it was of ſhort duration, as they were forced to leave him behind. During the corn feaſon he was employed in tending it, and not being of an impatient difpoſition, he bore his captivity without repining.

In the 7th month, 1781, the family went to Butlerſbury, when Col. Butler treated with the woman who was the head of this family for the releaſe of Abner, which ſhe at length confented to, on receiving ſome prefents, but faid he muſt firſt return with her, and ſhe would deliver him up in twenty days. Upon their return, ſhe gave Abner the agreeable information that he was to be given up. This added a ſpur to his induſtry, and made his labour light.

Some days before the time agreed on, they proceeded for Butlerſbury, and went

to

to John Secord's, where his fifter Elizabeth Gilbert had been from the time mentioned in the former part of this narrative.

Abner was difcharged by the Indians foon after his arrival at the Englifh village, and John Secord permitted him to live in his family with his fifter. With this family they continued two weeks, and as they were under the care of the Englifh officers, they were permitted to draw clothing and provifions from the king's ftores.

Afterwards Benj. Peart and his brother Thomas, who were both releafed, came over for their brother and fifter at John Secord's, and went with them to Capt. Powel's, in order to be nearer to the veffel they were to go in to Montreal.

The next of the family who comes within notice, is Elizabeth Gilbert, the fifter. From the time of her being firft introduced by the Indian into the family of John Secord, who was one in whom he placed great confidence. She was under the neceffity of having new clothes, as thofe fhe had brought from home were much worn. Her fituation in the family where fhe was placed was comfortable. After a few days refidence with them, fhe difcovered where the young child was, that had fome time before been taken from its mother Elizabeth Peart, as before-mentioned; and herfelf, together with John Secord's wife with
whom

whom she lived, and Capt. Fry's wife went to see it, in order to purchase it from the Indian woman who had it under her care; but they could not then prevail with her, though some time after Capt. Fry's wife purchased it for thirteen dollars. Whilst among the Indians it had been for a long time indisposed, and in a lingering distressing situation; but under its present kind protectress, who treated the child as her own, it soon recruited.

Elizabeth Gilbert, jun. lived very agreeably in J. Secord's family rather more than a year, and became so fondly attached to her benefactors, that she usually stiled the mistress of the house her mamma. During her residence here, her brother Abner, and Thomas Peart, came several times to visit her.

The afflicting loss of her father, to whom she was affectionately endeared, and the separation from her mother, whom she had no expectation of seeing again, was a severe trial, although moderated by the kind attentions shewn her by the family in which she lived.

John Secord having some business at Niagara, took Betsy with him, where she had the satisfaction of seeing six of her relations who had been captives, but were most of them released: this happy meeting made the trip to the fort a very agreeable one. She staid with them all night, and then returned.

D   Not

Not long after this vifit, Col. Butler and
John Secord fent for the Indian, who claimed
Elizabeth as his property, and when he arrived
they made overtures to purchafe her, but he
declared he would not fell his own flefh and
blood; for thus they ftile thofe whom they
have adopted. They then had recourfe to
prefents, which overcoming his fcruples,
they obtained her difcharge; after which fhe
remained two weeks at Butlerfbury, and
then went to her mother at Montreal.

Having given a brief relation of the happy
releafe and meeting of fuch of the captives
as had returned from among the Indians,
excepting Thomas Peart, whofe narrative
is deferred, as he was exerting his endeavours for the benefit of his fifter and coufin,
who ftill remained behind.

It may not be improper to return to the
mother, who with feveral of her children, were
at Montreal. The nurfe-child which they had
taken, as related in the former part of this
account, dying, was a confiderable lofs to
them, as they could not, even by their ut-
moft induftry, gain as much any other way.

In the fall of the year 1781, Col. Johnfon,
Capt. Powell, and fome other officers, came
to Montreal upon bufinefs, and were fo kind
in their remembrance of the family, as to
inquire after them, and to make them fome
prefents, congratulating the mother on the
happy

happy releafement of fo many of her children. They encouraged her with the information of their agreement with the Indians
for the releafement of her daughter Rebecca,
expecting that fhe was by that time at Niagara; but in this opinion they were mifta-
ken, as the Indian family who adopted her,
valued her too highly to be eafily prevailed
with, and it was a long time after this before
fhe was given up.

Elizabeth Gilbert and her daughters took
in clothes to wafh for their fupport, and being induftrious and careful, it afforded them
a tolerable fubfiftence.

Jeffe Gilbert obtained employ in his trade
as a cooper, which yielded a welcome addition to their ftock.

Elizabeth Gilbert fuffered no opportunity
to pafs her, of inquiring about her friends
and relations in Pennfylvania, and had the
fatisfaction of being informed, by one who
came from the fouthward, that friends of
Philadelphia had been very affiduous in
their endeavours to gain information where
their family was, and had fent to the different meetings, defiring them to inform themfelves of the fituation of the captivated family, and, if in their power, afford them fuch
relief as they might need.

It gave her great pleafure to hear of this
kind fympathizing remembrance of their
friends, and it would have been effentially

D 2   ferviceable

ferviceable to them, could they have reduced it to a certainty.

Deborah Jones, a daughter of Abraham Wing, a friend, fent for Elizabeth Gilbert, in order to attend her as a nurfe; but her death, which was foon after, fruftrated the profpect fhe had of an agreeable place, as this woman was better grounded in friends princi- ples than moft fhe had met with; which cir- cumftance united them in the ties of a clofe friendfhip : and as Eliz. Gilbert had received many civilities and favours from her, her death was doubly afflicting to their family.

A perfon who came from Crown-Point in- formed her that Benj. Gilbert, a fon of the deceafed by his firft wife, had come thither, in order to be of what fervice he could to the family, and had defired him to make inquiry where they were, and in what fituation, and fend him the earlieft information poffible.

A fecond agreeable intelligence fhe re- ceived from Niagara, by a young woman who came from thence, who informed her that her daughter Rebecca was given up to the Englifh by the Indians. This informa- tion muft have been very pleafing, as their expectations of her releafe were but faint; the Indian with whom fhe lived confidering her as her own child.

It was not long after this, that Thomas Peart, Rebecca Gilbert, and their coufin
Benjamin

Benjamin Gilbert, came to Montreal to the reft of the family. This meeting, after fuch fcenes of forrow as they had experienced, was more completely happy than can be exprefled.

Reflection, if indulged, will fteadily point out a protecting arm of power to have ruled the various ftorms which often threatened the family with deftruction on their paffage through the wildernefs, under the controul of the fierceft enemies, and preferved and reftored them to each other, although fepa-rated among different tribes and nations: this, fo great a favour, cannot be confider-ed by them but with the warmeft emotions of gratitude to the great Author.

Rebecca Gilbert and Benjamin Gilbert, jun. were feparated from their friends and connections at a place called the Five Mile Meadows, which was faid to be that diftance from Niagara. The Seneca king's daugh-ter, to whom they were allotted in the diftri-bution of the captives, took them to a fmall hut where her father Siangorochti, his queen, and the reft of the family were, eleven in number. Upon the reception of the prifon-ers into the family, there was much forrow and weeping, as is cuftomary upon fuch oc-cafions, and the higher in favour the adopt-ed prifoners are to be placed, the greater lamentation is made over them.

D 3

After

After three days the family removed to a place called the Landing, on the banks of Niagara River : here they continued two days more, and then two of the women went with the captives to Niagara, to procure clothing from the king's stores for them, and permitted them to ride on horseback to Fort Slusher, which is about eighteen miles distant from Niagara fort. On this journey they had a sight of the Great Falls of Niagara.

During a stay of six days at Fort Slusher, the British officers and others used their utmost endeavours to purchase them of the Indians : but the Indian king said he would not part with them for one thousand dollars.

The Indians who claimed Elizabeth Peart came to the fort with her at this time, and, although she was very weakly and indisposed, it was an agreeable opportunity to them both of conversing with each other; but they were not allowed to be frequently together, lest they should increase each other's discontent.

Rebecca being dressed in the Indian manner, appeared very different from what she had been accustomed to : short clothes, leggings, and a gold laced hat.

From Niagara fort they went about eighteen miles above the Falls to fort Erie, a garrison of the English, and then continued their journey about four miles further up Buffalo creek,

creek, and pitched their tent. At this place
they met with Rebecca's father and mother
by adoption, who had gone before on horfeback. They caught fome fifh, and made
foup of them; but Rebecca could eat none
of it, as it was dreffed without falt, and with
all the careleffnefs of Indians.

This fpot was intended for their plantation, they therefore began to clear the
land for the crop of Indian corn. While
the women were thus employed, the men
built a log-houfe for their refidence, and
then went out hunting.

Notwithftanding the family they lived
with was of the firft rank among the Indians,
and the head of it ftiled King, they were under the neceffity of labouring, as well as thofe
of lower rank, although they often had advantages of procuring more provifions than
the reft. This family raifed this fummer
about one hundred fkipple of Indian corn
(a fkipple is about three pecks) equal to fe-
venty-five bufhels.

As Rebecca was not able to purfue a courfe
of equal labour with the other women, fhe
was favoured by them by often being fent
into their hut to prepare fomething to eat;
and as fhe dreffed their provifions after the
Englifh method, and had erected an oven by
the affiftance of the other women, in which
they baked their bread, their family fared
more agreeably than the others.

D 4

Benjamin

Benjamin Gilbert, jun. was confidered as the king's fucceffor, and entirely freed from reftraint, fo that he even began to be delighted with his manner of life; and had it not been for the frequent counfel of his fellow captive, he would not have been anxious for a change.

In the waters of the lakes there are various kinds of fifh, which the Indians take fometimes with fpears; but whenever they can obtain hooks and lines, they prefer them.

A fifh called Ozoondah, refembling a fhad in fhape, but rather thicker, and lefs bony, with which Lake Erie abounded, was often dreffed for their table, and was of an agreeable tafte, weighing from three to four pounds.

They drew provifions this fummer from the forts, which frequently induced the Indians to repair thither. The king, his daughter, grand-daughter, and Rebecca, went together upon one of thefe vifits to Fort Erie, where the Britifh officers entertained them with a rich feaft, and fo great a profufion of wine, that the Indian king was very drunk; and as he had to manage the canoe in their return, they were repeatedly in danger of being overfet amongft the rocks in the lake.

Rebecca and Benjamin met with much better fare than the other captives, as the family they lived with were but feldom in great
want

want of neceſſaries, which was the only advantage they enjoyed beyond the reſt of their tribe.

Benjamin Gilbert, as a badge of his dignity, wore a ſilver medal pendant from his neck.

The king, queen, and another of the family, together with Rebecca and her couſin Benjamin, ſet off for Niagara, going as far as Fort Sluſher by water, from whence they proceeded on foot, carrying their loads on their backs. Their buſineſs at the fort was to obtain proviſions, which occaſioned them frequently to viſit it, as before related.

Rebecca indulged herſelf with the pleaſing expectation of obtaining her releaſe, or at leaſt permiſſion to remain behind among the whites; but in both theſe expectations ſhe was diſagreeably diſappointed, having to return again with her captors; all efforts for her releaſe being in vain. Col. Johnſon's houſekeeper, whoſe repeated acts of kindneſs to this captivated family have been noticed, made her ſome acceptable preſents.

As they had procured ſome rum to carry home with them, the chief was frequently intoxicated, and always in ſuch unhappy fits behaved remarkably fooliſh.

On their return, Thomas Peart, who was at Fort Niagara, procured for Rebecca an horſe to carry her as far as Fort Sluſher, where they took boat, and got home after a ſtay of nine days.

D 5   Soon

Soon after their return, Rebecca and her coufin were feized with the chill and fever, which held them for near three months. During their indifpofition the Indians were very kind to them; and as their ftrength of conftitution alone could not check the progrefs of the diforder, the Indians procured fome herbs, with which the patients were unacquainted, and made a plentiful decoction; with thefe they wafhed them, and it feemed to afford them fome relief: the Indians accounted it a fovereign remedy.

The deceafe of her father, of which Rebecca received an account, continued her in a drooping way a confiderable time longer than fhe would otherwife have been.

As foon as fhe recovered her health, fome of the family again went to Niagara, and Rebecca was permitted to be of the company. They ftaid at the fort about two weeks, and Col. Johnfon exerted himfelf in order to obtain her releafe, holding a treaty with the Indians for this purpofe; but his mediation proved fruitlefs: fhe had therefore to return with many an heavy ftep. When they came to Lake Erie, where their canoe was, they proceeded by water. While in their boat a number of Indians in a canoe came towards them, and informed them of the death of her Indian father, who had made an expedition to the frontiers of Pennfylvania, and was there wounded by the militia, and afterwards died

died of his wounds; on which occasion she was under the necessity of making a feint of forrow, and weeping aloud with the rest.

When they arrived at their settlement, it was the time of gathering their crop of corn, potatoes, pumpkins, and preserving their store of hickory nuts.

About the beginning of the winter some British officers came amongst them, and staid with them until spring, using every endeavour for the discharge of the two captives, but still unattended with success.

Some time after this another British officer, attended by Tho. Peart, came with provision and hoes for the Indians. It afforded them great happiness to enjoy the satisfaction of each other's conversation, after so long an absence.

Rebecca and her cousin had the additional pleasure of seeing her brother Abner, who came with the family amongst whom he lived, to settle near this place; and as they had not seen each other for almost twelve months, it proved very agreeable.

Thomas Peart endeavoured to animate his sister, by encouraging her with the hopes of speedily obtaining her liberty: but her hopes were often disappointed.

An officer amongst the British, one Capt. Latteridge, came and staid some time with them, and interested himself on behalf of the prisoners, and appeared in a fair way of obtaining their enlargement; but being ordered

to

to join his regiment, he was prevented from
further attention until his return from duty;
and afterwards was commanded by Col. Johnfon to go with him to Montreal on bufinefs
of importance, which effectually barred his
undertaking any thing further that winter.

It afforded her many pleafing reflections
when fhe heard that fix of her relations were
freed from their difficulties, and Tho. Peart
vifiting her again, contributed in fome meafure to re-animate her with frefh hopes of
obtaining her own freedom. They fixed
upon a fcheme of carrying her off privately;
but when they gave time for a full reflection,
it was evidently attended with too great
danger, as it would undoubtedly have much
enraged the Indians, and perhaps the lives of
every one concerned would have been for-
feited by fuch indifcretion.

During the courfe of this winter fhe fuffered many hardfhips and feveredifappointments,
and being without a friend to unbofom her
forrows to, they appeared to increafe by con-
cealment; but making a virtue of neceffity,
fhe fummoned up a firmnefs of refolution,
and was fupported under her difcouragement
beyond her own expectations.

The youth and inexperience of her coufin
did not allow of a fufficient confidence in
him, but fhe had often to intereft herfelf in
an attention to, and overfight of, his conduct; and it was in fome meafure owing to
this

this care, that he retained his defires to return amongft his friends.

Col. Butler fent a ftring of wampum to
the Indian chief, who immediately called a
number of the other Indians together upon
this occafion, when they concluded to go
down to Niagara, where they underftood the
defign of the treaty was for the freedom of
the remainder of the prifoners; for efpecial
orders were iffued by General Haldimand,
at Quebec, that their liberty fhould be obtained. At this Council-Fire it was agreed
they would furrender up the prifoners.

When they returned, they informed Rebecca that Col. Butler had a defire to fee
her, which was the only information fhe
could gain : this being a frequent cuftom
amongft them to offer a very flight furmife
of their intentions.

After this the whole family moved about
fix miles up Lake Erie, where they ftaid
about two months to gather their annual
ftore of maple fugar, of which they made a
confiderable quantity.

As foon as the feafon of this bufinefs was
over, they returned to their old fettlement,
where they had not continued long, before
an Indian came with an account that an afto-
nifhing number of young pigeons might be
procured at a certain place, by falling trees
that were filled with nefts of young, and the
diftance was computed to be about fifty
miles.

miles. This information delighted the feveral tribes: they fpeedily joined together,
young and old, from different parts, and
with great affiduit, purfued their expedition, and took abundance of the young ones,
which they dried in the fun, and with fmoke,
and filled feveral bags which they had taken
with them for this purpofe. Benjamin Gilbert was permitted to accompany them in
this excurfion, which muft have been a curious one for whole tribes to be engaged
in. On this rarity they lived with extra-
vagance for fome time, faring fumptuoufly
every day.

As the time approached, when, according
to appointment, they were to return to Niagara, and deliver up the prifoners, they gave
Rebecca the agreeable information, in order
to allow her fome time to make preparation. She made them bread for their journey with great cheerfulnefs.

The Indians, to the number of thirty, attended on this occafion with the two captives. They went as far as Fort Slufher
in a bark canoe. It was feveral days before they reached Niagara Fort, as they
went flowly on foot. After attending at
Col. Butler's, and conferring upon this occafion, in confideration of fome valuable
prefents made them, they releafed the two
laft of the captives, Rebecca Gilbert, and
Benjamin Gilbert, jun.

As

As fpeedily as they were enabled, their
Indian drefs was exchanged for the more
cuftomary and agreeable one of the Europeans; and on the third of the fixth month,
1782, two days after their happy releafe,
failed for Montreal.

The narrative of the treatment of Thomas Peart, another of the family, ftill remains to be given:

He was taken along the weftward path
with the prifoners before mentioned, viz.
Jofeph, Sarah, and Benjamin Gilbert, jun.

Thomas was compelled to carry a heavy
load of the plunder which the Indians had
feized at their farm. When feparated from
the reft, they were affured they fhould meet
together again in four days.

The firft day's travel was in an exceeding
difagreeable path, acrofs feveral deep brooks,
through which Thomas had to carry Sarah
and Benjamin Gilbert, jun. This tafk was
a very hard one, as he had been much reduced for want of fufficient nourifhment.

The firft night they lodged by the banks
of Cayuga Creek, the captives being tied as
ufual. The next morning they took a venifon, and this, with fome decayed corn
which they gathered from the deferted fields,
ferved them for fuftenance. This day's journey was by the fide of Cayuga Creek, until
they came to a fteep hill, which they afcended with difficulty.

When

When night came on, they fought a wigwam which had been deferted precipitately upon General Sullivan's march againft the inhabitants of thefe parts.

The land in this neighbourhood is excellent for cultivation, affording very good pafture.

Thomas Peart affured the Indians, that he, with the other captives, would not leave them, and therefore requefted the favour to be freed from their confinement at night; but one of them checked his requeft, by faying he could not fleep if the captives were fuffered to be untied.

Their meat being all exhaufted, Thomas and three Indians went near three miles to gather more decayed corn; and this, mouldy as it was, they were obliged to eat, it being their only food, excepting a few winter turnips which they met with. They went forwards a confiderable diftance by the fide of Cayuga Creek, and then with much difficulty croffed it; immediately afterwards they afcended an uncommon miry hill, covered with fprings. Going over this mountain they miffed the path, and were obliged to wade very heavily through the water and mire.

In the clofe of the day they came to a fine meadow, where they agreed to continue that night, having no other provifions than the mouldy Indian corn they accidentally met

with

with in the Indian plantations, which had been cut down, and left on the ground by General Sullivan's army.

Next morning they fet forwards, walking leifurely on, fo that the company who went by the other path might overtake them, and frequently ftopped for them.

When night approached, they came to a large creek where fome Indians were, who had begun to prepare the ground for planting corn. At this place they ftaid two nights, and being two indolent to procure game by hunting, their diet was ftill very poor, and their ftrength much exhaufted, fo that they became impatient of waiting for the others, which was their intention when they firft ftopped.

After travelling till near noon, they made a fhort ftay, ftripped the bark off a tree, and then painted, in their Indian manner, themfelves and the prifoners on the body of the tree; this done, they fet up a ftick with a fplit at the top, in which they placed a fmall bufh of leaves, and leaned the ftick fo that the fhadow of the leaves fhould fall to the point of the ftick where it was fixed in the ground; by which means the others would be directed in the time of day when they left the place.

Here they feparated the prifoners again, thofe to whom Thomas Peart and Jofeph
Gilbert.

Gilbert were allotted went weſtward out of the path, but Sarah Gilbert and Benjamin Gilbert, jun. with one Indian, continued in the path. This was very diſtreſſing to Sarah, to be torn from her relations, and deprived of all the comforts, and even neceſſaries of life. Theſe two, with the Indian who had the care of them, after they had parted with the other two, and travelled forward a few miles, came to ſome Indians by the ſide of a creek, who gave them ſomething to eat. The next day the Indian who was their pilot exerted himſelf to obtain ſome proviſions, but his endeavours proved fruitleſs; they therefore ſuffered greatly. At night the Indian aſked Sarah if ſhe had ever eaten horſe-fleſh, or dogs; ſhe replied, ſhe had not: he then further ſurpriſed her by aſking whether ſhe had ever eat man's fleſh; upon her expreſſing her abhorrence, he replied, that he ſhould be under the neceſſity of killing the boy, for he could not procure any deer. This threat, although perhaps not intended to be executed, terrified her exceedingly. He hunted with great diligence, leaving the captives by themſelves, and appeared to ſhudder himſelf at what he had threatened, willing to try every reſource; but notwithſtanding his exertions, her fears prevailed in a very great degree. They went forwards
ſlowly,

flowly, being very weak; and in addition to their diftrefs, there fell a very heavy rain, and they were obliged to continue in it, as they were without fhelter. In this reduced fituation they at length came to one of the huts at Canodofago, where they dreffed the remains of their mouldy corn, and the day after were joined by the part of the company whom they had left ten days before.

As the few days folitary fufferings of Sarah Gilbert had been before unrelated, the foregoing digreffion, from the narrative of Thomas Peart's, may not be thought improper.

To return to the two who were feparated from the path, and had to go forwards acrofs mountains and vallies, fwamps and creeks.

In the morning they eat the remainder of their corn. The Indians then cut off their hair, excepting a fmall round tuft on the crown of the head; and, after painting them in the Indian manner, in order to make them appear more terrible, they took from them their hats. Being thus obliged to travel bareheaded in the fun, they were feized with violent head-achs; and this, added to a want of provifions, was truly diftreffing.

When they approached the Indian fettlements, the Indians began their cuftomary whooping, to announce their arrival with prifoners; iffuing their difmal yells according to the number brought in.

After

After fome fhort time an Indian came to them: with him they held a difcourfe concerning the prifoners and painted them afrefh, part black, and part red, as a diftinguifhing mark. When this ceremony was concluded, the Indian who met them returned, and the others continued their route.

As they were not far from the Indian towns, they foon faw great numbers of the Indians collecting together, though the prifoners were ignorant of the motives.

When they came up to this difagreeable company, the Indian, who firft met them, took the ftring that was about Thomas Peart's neck, with which he had been tied at night, and held him whilft a Squaw ftripped off his veft.

Jofeph Gilbert was ordered to run firft, but being lame and indifpofed, could only walk. The clubs and tomahawks flew fo thick, that he was forely bruifed, and one of the tomahawks ftruck him on the head, and brought him to the ground, when a lad of about fifteen years old run after him, and, as he lay, would undoubtedly have ended him, as he had lifted the tomahawk for that purpofe, but the king's fon fent orders not to kill him.

After him, Thomas Peart was fet off; he feeing the horrid fituation of his brother, was fo terrified, that he did not recollect the

Indian

Indian still kept hold of the string which was round his neck; but, springing forwards with great force and swiftness, he pulled the Indian over, who, in return, when he recovered his feet, beat him severely with a club. The lad who was standing with a tomahawk near Joseph Gilbert, as he passed by him, threw his tomahawk with great dexterity, and would certainly have struck him, if he had not sprung forwards, and avoided the weapon. When he had got opposite to one of their huts, they pointed for him to take shelter there, where Joseph Gilbert came to him as soon as he recovered. In the room were a number of women, who appeared very sorrowful, and wept aloud; this, though customary amongst them, still added to the terror of the captives, as they imagined it to be no other than a prelude to inevitable destruction.

Their hair cropped close, their bodies bruised, and the blood gushing from Joseph Gilbert's wound, rendered them a horrid spectacle to each other.

After the lamentation ceased, one of them asked Thomas Peart, if he was hungry; he replied, he was: they then told him, "You eat by and by." They immediately procured some victuals, and set it before them; but Joseph Gilbert's wounds had taken away his appetite.

An

An officer, who was of the French families of Canada, came to them, and brought a negro with him to interpret. After queſtioning them, he concluded to write to Col. Johnſon at Niagara, relative to the priſoners.

The Indians adviſed them to be contented with their preſent ſituation, and marry amongſt them, giving every aſſurance that they ſhould be treated with the utmoſt reſpect: but theſe conditions were inadmiſſible.

After this, Joſeph Gilbert was taken from his brother, as related in the narrative of his ſufferings.

Thomas Peart continued at the village that night, and the next day was given to the care of a young Indian, who went with him about two miles, where ſeveral Indians were collected, dreſſed in horrid maſks, in order, as he ſuppoſed, to make ſport of his fears, if he diſcovered any: he therefore guarded againſt being ſurpriſed, and when they obſerved him not to be intimidated, they permitted him to return again. Not long after arriving at the village, Capt. Rowland Monteur came in, who gave Thomas Peart ſome account how the others of his family had ſuffered, and told him that he had almoſt killed his mother and Jeſſe, on account of Andrew Harrigar's making his eſcape. He had come in before the others, in order to procure

procure some provisions for the company, who were in great need of it.

When the Captain returned, Tho. Peart accompanied him part of the way, and the Captain advised him to be cheerful and contented, and work faithful for the friend, for so he ftiled the Indian under whose care Thomas Peart was placed, promising him that if he complied, he should shortly go to Niagara.

They employed him in chopping for several days, having previous to this taken the ftring from his neck, which they had carefully secured him with every night.

The plantation on which they intended to fix for a summer residence, and to plant their crop of corn, was several miles down the Genesee, or Little River. Prior to their removing with the family, some of the men went thither, and built a bark hut, which was expeditiously performed, as they executed it in about two days, when they returned to their old habitation.

Thomas Peart was the next day given to the chief Indian, who endeavoured to quiet his apprehensions, affuring him he should meet with kind treatment.

The Indian manner of life is remarkably dirty and loufy; and although they themselves disregard their filth, yet it was extremely mortifying to the prisoners to be

deprived

deprived of the advantages of cleanliness; and this was by no means among the number of smaller difficulties.

As Thomas Peart had been accustomed to industry, and when first among the Indians was constantly exerting himself, either in their active diversions or useful labour, they were much delighted with him. When they had concluded upon sending him to the family he was to reside with, they daubed him afresh with their red paint. He was then taken about seven miles, where he was adopted into the family, and stiled " Och-" nusa," or uncle. When the ceremony of adoption was performed, a number of the relatives were summoned together, and the head of them took Thomas Peart into the midst of the assembly, and made a long harangue in the Indian language. After this he was taken into the house, where the women wept aloud for joy, that the place of a deceased relation was again supplied.

The old man, whose place Thomas Peart was to fill, had never been considered by his family as possessed of any merit; and, strange as it may appear, the person adopted always holds, in their estimation, the merits or demerits of the deaeased, and the most careful conduct can never overcome this prejudice.

As soon as the ceremony of adoption at this place was finished, he was taken by the
family

family to Nundow, a town on the Genefee
River. The head of this family was a chief
or king of the Senecas. But before Thomas
was fully received into the family, there was
a fecond lamentation.

Their provifions, notwithftanding it was
a feafon of great plenty, was often deers guts,
dried with the dung, and all boiled together,
which they confider ftrong and wholefome
food. They never throw away any part of
the game they take.

Thomas Peart's drefs was entirely in the
Indian ftile, painted and ornamented like
one of themfelves, though in a meaner manner, as they did not hold him high in efteem
after his adoption.

Greatly difcontented, he often retired into
the woods, and reflected upon his unhappy
fituation, without hopes of returning to his
relations, or ever being refcued from captivity.

He continued in this folitary feclufion
about five weeks, when their corn was moft-
ly confumed; and as their dependence for a
frefh fupply was on Niagara fort, they concluded to go thither, but at firft would not
confent that Thomas fhould accompany
them; but he was fo urgent, they at length
confented, and the next day they had an Indian dance, preparatory to their expedition.

In the route Thomas Peart got a deer,
which was an acceptable acquifition, as they

had

had been for fome days without any meat, and their corn was likewife expended.

When they came within two miles of the fort, they halted, and ftaid there until morning.

A white prifoner, who came from the fort, gave Thomas Peart a particular relation of his fellow captives: this was the firft account he had of them fince their feparation at the Indian towns. As foon as he came to the fort, he applied to fome of the officers, requefting their exertions to procure Thomas's liberty, if poffible; but he was difappointed, as nothing could be then done to ferve him.

He eat fome falt provifions, which, as he had tafted but little falt fince his captivity, (although pleafing to his palate) affected his ftomach, it being difficult for him to digeft.

As he was to return with the Indians in about a week, it was very diftreffing, being much difgufted with the fare he met amongft them.

They returned by way of Fort Slufher, and then along Lake Erie, up Buffalo Creek, taking fome fifh as they went. They paffed by the place where Elizabeth Peart and Rebecca Gilbert were, but he had not an opportunity of feeing them.

The ftores they took home with them, confifted of rum, falt, and ammunition.

Lake

Lake Erie is about three hundred miles long from eaſt to weſt, and about forty in breadth: it receives its ſupply of waters from Lakes Superior, Michigan, and Huron, by a North Weſt paſſage, called the Streights of Detroit. A very long narrow piece of land lies on its north ſide, which projects remarkably into the lake, and has been noticed by moſt travellers, and is known by the name of Long Point. There are ſeveral iſlands in it, which, with the banks of the lake, were more infeſted with different kinds of ſnakes, particularly the rattle-ſnake, than other places.

The navigation of this lake is allowed to be more dangerous than the others, on account of the high lands projecting into it; ſo that when ſudden ſtorms ariſe, boats are frequently loſt, as there are but few places to land, and ſeldom a poſſibility of finding a ſhelter near the craggy precipices.

The waters of Erie paſs through a northeaſt communication into the river Niagara, which, by a northerly courſe of near thirty-ſix miles, falls into Lake Ontario.

At the diſcharge of this river into Lake Ontario, on the eaſt ſide, ſtands Fort Niagara; and at the entrance from Lake Erie lies Erie Fort; between theſe two forts are thoſe extraordinary falls which claim the attention

E 2   tention

tention of the curious, and are amongſt the moſt remarkable works of nature.

This ſtupendous cataract is ſupplied with the waters of the ſeveral lakes, and their diſtant ſprings; which, after traverſing many hundred miles, ruſh aſtoniſhingly down a moſt horrid precipice, and which, by a ſmall iſland, is ſeparated into two large columns, and each near one hundred and forty feet perpendicular, and in a ſtrong, rapid, inconceivable foam and roar, extends near nine miles further, having in this diſtance a deſcent nearly equal to the firſt.

The ſtreight of Niagara is eſteemed dangerous for a mile or upwards above the falls. The water of the falls raiſes a very heavy miſt, ſomewhat reſembling a continuation of the river; and this deception, together with the rapidity of the current, frequently hurries the ducks and geeſe down this dreadful precipice.

This vaſt body of water, after paſſing through the Streight of Niagara, is received by Lake Ontario, or Cataraqui, which is nearly of an oval form. Its greateſt length is from north-eaſt to ſouth-weſt, and is generally allowed to be ſix hundred miles in circumference. And although the leaſt of the five great lakes of Canada is much the ſafeſt for ſhipping, as the channel is leſs obſtructed by rocks or iſlands, than

the

the other lakes. The fouth fide is the moft commodious for batteaux and canoes, having a moderately fhelving bank and fhore on that fide: the other is more rocky.

Many of the rivers which fall into it are barred in their entrances by broken hills, but the vallies are uncommonly fertile.

On the fouth the moft confiderable rivers which fall into this lake, are, the great and little Seneca. The falls of thefe rivers render them not navigable near the lake; but after the carrying-places are paffed, they run flow and deep.

In order to keep up the communication between the different parts of Canada, there is a portage from the landing below Niagara Falls, to the landing above, up three fharp hills, along which, the road for about eight or nine miles has been made as eafy for carts as it poffibly could; (thence to Lake Erie is about eighteen miles) but the ftream is fo fwift here, that it is almoft impoffible to ftem it for a mile or two in a fhip with the ftiffeft gale; though batteaux and canoes pafs along without much danger, as the current is lefs rapid near the fhore. On the north-eaft it empties itfelf into the river Cataraqui.

From this fhort digreffive account of the lakes, we may return to the fituation of the prifoner, and the Indian family.

E 3   When

When they had confumed their laft year's ftock of corn, they lived very low, and were reduced to great neceffity, digging what wild efculent roots they could find; this was fo different from what he had been accuftomed to, that he could not bear it with that cheerfulnefs with which the Indians met fuch difficulties. His painful reflections, and the want of neceffaries, reduced him exceeding low.

Whilft in this diftrefs, he happily obtained the ufe of a teftament from a white woman, who had been taken captive, and afterwards married amongft them. With this folacing companion, he frequently retired into the woods, and employed himfelf in reading and meditating upon the inftruction couched in it.

The Indians directed a white girl to inform him, that they intended a hunt of twenty days, and were defirous he fhould attend them; to this he agreed, and the whole family accompanied the hunters. They paffed by the town where Jofeph Gilbert was, who informed his brother that he was going to Niagara: Thomas Peart replied he had already been there, and then informed him how the others of their relations were difperfed.

On their way up the Genefee River, where they intended to hunt, they took a deer.

The

The fourth day, as Thomas Peart was beating for game, he loft his company; but at length came to fome Indians, who directed him. When he came to the family much fatigued, and told them he had been loft, they were much delighted at the perplexing fituation he had been in.

The next day they moved further, hunting as they went, and in the evening fixed their quarters, where they ftaid two nights.

Thomas Peart not endeavouring to pleafe them, they took umbrage at his neglect. This, added to a fit of the ague, induced them to leave him in the woods, he being fo weak he could not keep up with them, and was obliged to follow by their tracks in the leaves.

Their provifions foon began to wafte, and it was not long before it was entirely confumed; and as they took no game, they were under the neceffity of eating wild cherries.

The profpect appeared very gloomy to our captive, to be thus diftreffed with hunger, and to be from home near one hundred miles with the whole family: but this fituation, though fo alarming to him, did not appear to reach their ftoic infenfibility. In this extremity one of the Indians killed a fine elk, which was a long wifhed-for and delightful fupply; but as the weather was very warm,

and

and they had no falt, it foon became putrid, and filled with maggots, which they, not-withftanding, eat without referve.

After they had been out upwards of thirty days, the Indians changed their courfe towards their own habitation, making but little progrefs forwards, as they kept hunting as they went. And as Thomas had long been uneafy, and defirous to return, not expecting to have been abfent more than twenty days, they gave him fome directions, and a fmall fhare of provifions; he then left them, after an unfuccefsful hunt of forty days: and, although weak and unfit for the journey, he fet off in the morning, and kept as near a north-weft courfe as he could, going as faft as his ftrength would permit over large creeks, fwamps, and rugged hills; and when night came on, made up a fmall fire, and being exceedingly fatigued, laid himfelf down on the ground, and flept very foundly. In the morning he continued his journey.

When he confidered the great diftance through the woods to the Indian towns, and the difficulty of procuring game to fubfift on, it dejected him greatly. His fpirits were fo depreffed, that when his fire was extinguifhed in the night, he even heard the wild beafts walking and howling around him, without regarding them, as with all his

his exertions and assiduity, he had but small hope of ever reaching the towns, but providentially he succeeded.

On the journey he eat a land tortoise, some roots and wild cherries.

When he reached the town, the Indians were pleased with his return, and inquired the reason of his coming alone, and where he had left the family he went with; which he fully informed them of.

This being the time for feasting on their new crop of corn, and they having plenty of pumpkins and squashes, gave an agreeable prospect of a short season of health, and frequent, though simple, feasts.

About ten days after this, the family returned; they soon inquired if Thomas Peart had reached home, and upon being informed that he had, replied that it was not expected he ever could.

The Indians concluding to make a war excursion, asked Thomas to be with them; but he determinately refused them, and was therefore left at home with the family; and not long after had permission to visit his brother Benjamin Peart, who was then about fifteen or eighteen miles distant, down the Genesee river.

Benjamin Peart was at that time very much indisposed: Thomas, therefore, staid with him several days, and, when he reco-

vered

vered a little ftrength, left him, and returned
to his old habitation.

He was thoroughly acquainted with the
cuftoms, manners, and difpofitions of the
Indians, and obferving that they treated him
juft as they had done the old worthlefs Indian, in whofe place he was adopted, (he
having been confidered a perquifite of the
Squaws ;) he therefore concluded he would
only fill his predeceffor's ftation, and ufed no
endeavours to pleafe them, as his bufinefs
was to cut wood for the family; notwithftanding he might eafily have procured a fufficient ftore, yet he was not fo difpofed, but
often refufed, and even left it for the Squaws
fometimes to do themfelves, not doubting, if
he was diligent and careful, they would be
lefs willing to give him his liberty.

Jofeph Gilbert came to fee him, and, as
has been mentioned, informed him of the deceafe of their father.

Some time in the fall, the king (whofe
brother Thomas was called) died, and he was
directed to hew boards, and make a coffin for
him; when it was completed, they fmeared
it with red paint. The women, whofe attention to this is always infifted on amongft the
Indians, kept the corpfe for feveral days,
when they prepared a grave, and interred
him; it being confidered amongft this tribe
difgraceful for a man to take any notice of
this

this folemn and interefting fcene. A number of Squaws collected upon this occafion,
and there was great mourning, which they
continued for feveral days at ftated times.
As the place of interment, as well as that
appointed for weeping, was near the hut
Thomas Peart refided at, he had an opportunity of indulging his curiofity, through the
openings of the logs, without giving of-
fence.

Soon after this, one of the women, who
was called Thomas's fifter, defired him to
accompany her about fifty miles towards
Niagara. Some others of the family went
with them, and in their way they took a deer
and other game.

They were from home on this journey
about fix days; during the time, there fell a
very heavy fnow, which made their journey
toilfome. The women were fent homeward
before the reft, to prepare fomething againft
they came.

When they had loitered at home a few
days, they fet about gathering their winter
ftore of hickory nuts: from fome of them
they extracted an oil, which they eat with
bread or meat, at their pleafure.

Frequently before they fet off on their
hunting parties, they make an Indian frolick;
when, commonly, all the company become
extravagantly intoxicated: and when they in-

E 6   tend

tend to go off this winter, they firſt give the preparatory entertainment.

After they were gone, Thomas Peart and the miſtreſs of the family diſagreeing, ſhe inſiſted upon his joining to the hunters, and living on the game, that ſhe might ſave more corn. He pleaded the coldneſs of the ſeaſon, and his want of clothing, but it would not avail; he was therefore turned out, and upon finding the hunters, he built them huts, where they ſtaid for ſome weeks, taking the game, and eating wild meat without corn, as the ſupply they had raiſed was ſhort.

When they were weary with their employ, they moved to their old hut, and lived in their idle manner for a long time. They then again returned to their hut, and ſtaid about ten days, and took ſeveral deer.

A few days after their return from hunting, they acquainted Thomas that they ſhould ſet off for Niagara; which was truly grateful to him. There were fifteen of them on this viſit. The old woman gave Thomas Peart a ſtrict charge to return.

Although the proſpect of ſeeing or hearing from his relations was delightful, yet the journey was exceſſively painful; the ſnow covering the ground to a conſiderable depth, the cold increaſed, and they had to wade through ſeveral deep creeks, the water often freezing to their legs; and Thomas Peart, as

well

well as the reft, were unclothed, excepting a
blanket and pair of leggings.

In five days they came to Fort Slufher,
and at the treats they there received, were
moft of them drunk for the day.

Next morning they went to Niagara, where
he immediately made application to the Britifh officers to folicit his releafe. Captain
Powel informed Colonel Johnfon, who requefted it of the Indians; they required fome
time to deliberate upon the fubject, not willing to difoblige the Colonel, and at length
concluded to comply with his requeft; telling him, that however hard it might be to
part with their own flefh, yet, to pleafe him,
they confented to it, hoping he would make
them fome prefent.

Colonel Johnfon then directed him to his
own houfe, and defired him to clean himfelf,
and fent clothes for him to drefs with. Here
he had plenty of falt provifions, and every
neceffary of life: this, with the happy regain-
ing of his liberty, gave a new fpring to his
fpirits, and, for a few days, he fcarcely knew
how to enjoy fufficiently this almoft unlook-
ed-for change.

When recruited, he went to work for
Colonel Johnfon, and a few weeks after had
the fatisfaction of his brother Benjamin Peart's
company; who, though not releafed, yet was
permitted to ftay at the fort, and worked with
his

his brother until spring; when Capt. Powel, Lieutenant Johnson, and Thomas Peart went up Buffalo Creek, with two boats loaded with provisions, and a proportion of planting corn, together with hoes, to be distributed among the Indians.

In this expedition Thomas had the satisfaction of seeing and conversing with his sister Rebecca, which was the first of their meeting together, after a separation of a year.

At the distribution of the corn and hoes, the Indians met, and made a general feast; after which they dispersed; and the officers, when they had completed their business, returned to Niagara, after an absence of eight or nine days.

Thomas Peart was settled at Col. Johnson's to work for him at two shillings and sixpence per day, till the eighth month, when six of the captives were sent to Montreal, and Thomas also had permission to go, but he chose rather to stay, to afford his assistance to his sister Rebecca Gilbert, and his cousin Benjamin Gilbert, junior, who yet remained in captivity; exerting himself as strenuously as possible on their behalf.

In the fall, he went up again to Buffalo Creek, where he saw his sister and cousin a second time, and assured his sister that the Colonel intended to insist on her being releafed; this encouraged her to hope.

The

The Indians are too indolent to employ fufficient pains to preferve their grain in the winter; therefore, thofe who plant near the fort, generally fend the greater part to the Englifh to preferve for them, and take it back as they want it: therefore, what this neighbourhood had more than for a fhort fupply, they carried with them in their boats to the fort.

In the winter, Thomas Peart undertook to chop wood for the Britifh officers, and built himfelf a hut about two miles from the fort, in which he lodged at night. A drunken Indian came to his cabin one evening with a knife in his hand, with an intention of mifchief; but, being debilitated with liquor, Thomas Peart eafily wrefted his knife from him.

A wolf came one night up to the door of his cabin, which he difcovered next morning, by the tracks in the fnow; and a few nights after paid a fecond vifit, when he fired at him, and, by the blood on the fnow, fuppofed he had mortally wounded him.

Next fpring, Thomas went with the officers again up Buffalo Creek, when he afrefh animated his fifter, by informing her that General Haldimand had given orders to the officers to procure their liberty.

As they returned by Fort Erie, their boats were in danger from the ice in the lake and river,

river. It continues in thefe parts until late in the fpring; fometimes as late as the fifth month; and, as foon as melted, the vegetation is aftonifhingly quick.

About two weeks after they returned, Thomas Peart went back again with fome officers, who were going to the Indians.

After a tour of fifteen days, he came again to the fort, where he ftaid for feveral weeks, and received feveral letters from his relations at Montreal, by fome officers who were on their way to Cataraguors, on Lake Erie, about eighty miles from Niagara; who, in their way, faw Rebecca and Benjamin Gilbert, jun. with a number of Indians, going for Niagara. Tho. Peart made as quick difpatch as poffible to meet them, delighted with the profpect of their obtaining their liberty.

They took a porcupine, which is fomewhat larger than a rackoon, and covered remarkably with quills of bone, about eight or nine inches long, which they can difcharge with fuch force, as to penetrate through a man's hand at a confiderable diftance.

A few days after he returned from this expedition, the captives were delivered up: thefe two had been with the Indians upwards of two years.

In a fhort time after their releafe, Thomas Peart procured permiffion for them and himfelf to proceed to Montreal, and was furnifhed

ed with a pafs, containing an order to obtain what provifions they might be in want
of in their paffage.

The fecond day of the 6th month, 1782,
they went on board the fhip Limner, and proceeded towards Montreal. When they came
againft the place where their father was interred, thofe whom they were with gave Thomas and Rebecca notice, though they did
not land, but purfued their voyage; and,
after being feven days on the water, they
reached Fort Lafheen, where they ftaid that
night, and the next day went to Montreal to
their relations: foon after which, a letter was
received from the before-mentioned Benj.
Gilbert, then at Caftleton, acquainting them
of his being fo far on his way to Montreal,
in order to give them affiftance in getting
home, and requefting that permiffion might
be obtained for his coming in; which Elizabeth immediately applied to the officers for:
who with great cheerfulnefs wrote in her behalf to Gen. Haldimand, at Quebec, who
readily granted her requeft, together with
other favours to Elizabeth, worthy of her
grateful remembrance; by which means Benjamin's arrival at Montreal was foon effect-
ed, where he had the pleafure once more of
feeing and converfing with his relations and
neareft connexions, to their great joy and fatisfaction, after an abfence of near three years;
during

during which time, they had but little if any certain account of each other.

· After some time spent in inquiring after their relatives and friends, and conversing on the once unthought of and strange scenes of life they had passed through since their separation, it became necessary to prepare for their journey homewards, which was accordingly done; and in about five weeks from the time of Benjamin's arrival, they took leave of the friends and acquaintances they had made during their residence there, whose hospitable and kind treatment merits their grateful and sincere acknowledgments, and most ardent desires for their welfare in every scene. And on the 22d day of the 8th month, 1782, attended by a great number of the inhabitants, they embarked in boats prepared for them, and took their departure. Having crossed the river, and carriages being provided, they proceeded on their journey without much delay, until they came to St. John's, where they went on board a sloop; but the winds being unfavourable, rendered their passage in the lake somewhat tedious.

They did not arrive at Crown-Point until about two weeks after their departure from Montreal. They continued here several days, and from thence went in open boats to East-Bay in about two days, where they landed and staid all night, and were next day delivered

up

up to the officers of Vermont. Here fome of the company ftaid two nights, on account of Benjamin Peart's child being very ill; by which time it fo recovered, that they proceeded on to Caftleton, where thofe that went before had halted, and near that place ftaid all night, and in the morning Elizabeth, the mother, having engaged to do an errand for a friend, was under a neceflity of riding about thirty-five miles, which occafioned her to be abfent two nights from the family, who were at Captain Willard's; at which place Benjamin provided horfes and waggons for the remainder of the journey, together with fome provifions. Here they were very civilly treated, and generoufly entertained, free of expence.

The family then proceeded on, and met their mother at the houfe of Captain Lanfon, where they ftaid that night and until noon next day, and were alfo kindly treated by him.

Continuing their journey, they met with John Bracanage (who, together with Captain Lanfon, were paffengers with them to Eaft-Bay); he gave them an invitation to his houfe, which they accepted, and arrived there about noon next day, and continued with him two nights, and were refpectfully entertained.

Having prepared for profecuting their journey, they proceeded on for the North-River, where they met with Lot Trip and William

William Knowles, who kindly conducted
the women to the houſe of David Sands,
where they lodged that night. The reſt of
the family came to them in the morning,
and ſeveral of them attended friends meeting, not having had the like opportunity
for ſeveral years before.

In the afternoon they purſued their journey,
the before-mentioned Lot Trip and William
Knowles accompanying them, and being in
a waggon, kindly took Elizabeth and her
younger daughter paſſengers with them,
which proved a conſiderable relief.

In a few days they came into Pennſylvania,
where they met with ſome of their relations,
and former acquaintances and friends, who
were unitedly rejoiced at the happy event of
once more ſeeing and converſing with them.

The next day, being the twenty-eighth day
of the ninth month, 1782, they arrived at
Byberry, the place of their nativity, and the
reſidence of their neareſt connexions and
friends, where Elizabeth and her children
were once more favoured with the agreeable
opportunity of ſeeing and converſing with
her ancient mother, together with their other
neareſt relatives and friends, to their mutual
joy and ſatisfaction; under which happy cir-
cumſtance we now leave them.

THOUGHTS

THOUGHTS

Alluding to, and in Part occafioned by,
the CAPTIVITY and SUFFERINGS of
BENJAMIN GILBERT and his
FAMILY.

A S from the foreſt iſſues the fell boar,
    So human ravagers, in deſerts bred,
On the defenceleſs, peaceful hamlet pour
    Wild waſte o'er all, and ſudden ruin ſpread !

Here, undiſguis'd, war's brutal ſpirit ſee,
    Its venom'd nature to the root laid bare,
In which (trick'd up in webs of policy)
    Profeſſing Chriſtians vindicate their ſhare.

Pompous profeſſion, vaunting in a name,
    Floats lightly on an oſtentatious ſhow,
Nor dips ſincere, in reſignation's ſtream,
    To bring memorials from the depths below.

Sophiſticated dogmas of the ſchools,
    The flatulent, unwholeſome food of ſtrife,
With zeal pedantic for tradition's rules,
    Still crucify the principle of life.

The

The woes of this probationary ftate,
    Through life fo mingled and diverfified,
Derive their chief malignity and weight
    From murm'ring difcontent and captious pride.

Tranfient is human life, all flefh as grafs,
    The goodlinefs of man but as a flow'r.
Fine gold muft through the fervid furnace pafs;
    Through death we immortality explore.

Through judgment muft deliverance be known,
    From vile affections, and their wrathful fting;
True peace pertains to righteoufnefs alone,
    That flows, through faith, from life's eternal fpring!

Should man (to glory call'd, and endlefs blifs)
    Bewail his momentary adverfe doom!
Or in deep thankful refignation kifs
    The rod that prompts him on his journey home?

Unfearchable the providence of God,
    By boafted wifdom of the fon of duft;
Lo! virtue feels oppreffion's iron rod,
    And impious fpirits triumph o'er the juft.

Shall hence a felf-conceited reptile dare
    Th' omnifcient Ruler's equity arraign?
Say here thy wrath is fit, thy bounty there,
    Good to promote, and evil to reftrain.

Believing fouls unfeignedly can fay,
    Not mine, by thy all-perfect will be done;
If beft this bitter cup fhould pafs away,
    Or be endur'd, to thee, not me, is known.

Deep

Deep tribulation in the humbly wife,
 Through patience to divine experience leads;
The ground where hope fecurely edifies,
 Purg'd of the filth whence confcious fhame proceeds.

Affliction is Bethefda's cleanfing pool,
 Deep fearching each diftemper of the mind;
The poor way-farer, though efteem'd a fool,
 Baptizing here, immortal health may find.

Though for the prefent grim adverfity
 Not joyous is, but grievous to fuftain;
Humblin the fhepherd's call—"Come learn of me"
 In lowly meeknefs to endure thy pain.

Yet fhall it work a glorious recompence;
 Nor can the heart of man conceive in full,
The good by infinite Benificence,
 Stor'd for the patient unrepining foul.

Some feeble ones fuftain the galling yoke,
 With firmnefs, no ferocious tempers know;
Calm refignation mitigates the ftroke
 Of ills, tremendous to the diftant view!

If difappointment blaft thy fanguine hope,
 Indulg'd in fublunary profpects fair,
Conclude thy guardian angel made the ftop,
 To check thy blind, thy dangerous career.

The captive family in favage bonds,
 Trace through each rugged way and tracklefs wild:
Through famine, toils unknown, and hoftile wounds,
 The tender mother with her infant child.

Then

Then with thy lighter-griefs their forrows weigh,
   Nor let thy own demerits be forgot :
Impartial inference deduce, and fay
   · Whence thy exemption from their heavy lot :

Is it thy wifdom fhields thee in the hour,
   When mighty dangers o'er thy head impend ?
Can thine, or other mortal arm of power,
   From famine, peftilence, or ftorm defend ?

Confefs 'tis mercy covers thee from harm,
   A care benign, unmerited by thee ;
And if the grateful fenfe thy bofom warm,
   Small price is paid for fuch felicity.

If the hard Indian's wild ferocity,
   Againft their race thy indignation move,
Think on the example due to them from thee,
   Profeffing Chriftian equity and love.

So fhall their cruel, their abhorred deeds,
   Inftruction to the humble mind convey ;
Remind us whence all violence proceeds,
   And ftrengthen to purfue the peaceful way.

Vengeance with vengeance holds perpetual war :
   Love only can o'er enmity prevail ;
Sulphur and pitch, abfurdly who prepare,
   To quench devouring fire, are fure to fail.

Hear ye vindictive ! -be no longer proud,
   The high decree is paft, gone forth the word ;
No vain illufion————'tis the voice of God !
   " Who ufe the fword muft perifh by the fword."

                                 Perifh

Perifh from that divine ennobling fenfe
   Of heavenly good, which evil overcomes;
That light, whofe energetic influence,
   With piercing ray difpels bewild'ring glooms.

From whence come mortal jarrings! come they, not
   From luft, from pride, from felfifh arrogance?
In which, from peace and freedom far remote,
   The blind goad on the blind, a flavifh dance.

What! cries the zealot, fhall not Chriftian faith
   O'er heathen infidelity prevail ?
—Yes——but the means is not thy will, thy wrath ;
   Means which confederate with death and hell.

Did ever tyger-hearted Spanifh chief,
   By thofe dire maffacres in ftory told,
Vanquifh Peruvia's ftubborn unbelief,
   Or add one convert to the Chriftian fold?

Vindictive man will ftill retaliate,
   Evil for evil, and ftill rack his brains,
For arguments the caufe to vindicate ;
   Nor knows what fpirit in his bofom reigns.

Meffiah is the love of God to man !
   Reveal'd on earth, not to deftroy, but fave ;
By wifdom's peaceful influence to maintain,
   Dominion over death, hell, and the grave.

But why for Chriftian purity contend ?
   Who hath, alas ! believ'd the glad report ?
How many boaft the name, the name defend ;
   Yet make the virtual life their fcoff and fport ?

F   Deal

Deal forth their cenfures with unfparing zeal,
   'Gainft favage violence and cruel wrong ;
N̈ȯr dream the real effental infidel
   Holds o'er their fpirits his dominion ftrong.

What Turkifh rover, or what heathen foe,
   Shews more contempt of gofpel equity,
Than thofe, to fultry climes remote who go,
   T' enflave their fellow men, by nature free ?

The yelling warrior, with relentlefs hand,
   Leaves parent childlefs, fatherlefs the fon ;
Their griefs our tender fympathy demand ;
   But what have diftant Afric's children done ?

Will ftill the pick-thank, temporizing prieft,
   Give this oppreffion Pharifaic aid ?
Will civiliz'd believers ftill perfift
   To vindicate the abominable trade ?

Th' extenfive, deep, unrighteous t' unfold,
   Weft-India's dark, inhuman laws explore ;
What grofs iniquity we there behold,
   In folemn acts of legiflative pow'r ?

Britons, who loud for liberty contend,
   Affect to guard their nation from the ftain ;
Yet fordidly in Mammon's temple bend,
   And largely fhare in the ungodly gain.

What ardent execrations do we hear,
   'Gainft barb'rous Mohoc's, bloody Shawanefe ?
From father's arms their hopeful fons who tear ;
   From mother's breafts love's tender pledges feize.

                    O Chriftian !

O Chriftian! think with what redoubled force,
　'Gainft which fallacious artifice is vain,
On thee recurs thy aggravated curfe,
　　Heav'n's righteous Judge pronouncing,
　　　　art the man."

Think for what end the Mediator came,
　On earth an ignominious death to die ;
Thy foul from wrath's dominion to redeem,
　And to himfelf a people purify.

Books printed and fold by James Phillips.

THE Select Works of William Penn, in five
　　Volumes 8vo. Price 2s. 6d. well bound, or 25s.
in Calf, lettered.

　Fruits of Solitude, in Reflections and Maxims relating to the Conduct of Human Life, in Two Parts,
by William Penn. To which is added,
　Fruits of a Father's Love, being the Advice of Wm.
Penn to his Children, relating to their Civil and Religious Conduct, very fmall fize, bound, 2s. 6d.

　The Works of Isaac Pennington, in Four Volumes 8vo. well bound, 20s. Calf lettered 22s.

　An Apology for the True Chriftian Divinity, by
Robert Barclay, 5s. On SuperfineWriting Paper,
large 8vo.

The Sacred Hiſtory of the Old and New Teſtament, by Thomas Ellwood, Three Volumes 8vo. well bound, 15s.

An Account of the Goſpel Labours and Chriſtian Labours of a faithful Miniſter in Chriſt, John Churchman, late of Nottingham in Pennſylvania, deceaſed, 8vo. bound 4s.

A Journal of the Life, Travels, and Labours, in the Work of the Miniſtry, of John Griffith, 8vo. bound 2s. 6d.

Some Conſiderations relating to the preſent State of the Chriſtian Religion, &c. by Alexander Arscott, 8vo. bound 3s.

Select Poems, &c. occaſionally written on various Subjects. To which is added, the Hiſtory of the Prophets Elijah and Eliſha, a Poem, by John Fry, bound 1s. 6d.

A Journal of the Life of John Grattan, 8vo. bound 2s.

God's Protecting Providence Man's ſureſt Help and Defence; evidenced in the remarkable Deliverance of Robert Barrow, and others. By Jonathan Dickenſon. New Edition, 1s.

An Account of the Captivity of Elizabeth Hanſon, late of Kachecky, in New England, 3d.